fangirl

by
Ken Baker

RP|KIDS
PHILADELPHIA • LONDON

For My Family

Books published by Running Press are available at special discounts for bulk
purchases in the United States by corporations, institutions, and other organizations.
For more information, please contact the Special Markets Department at the
Perseus Books Group, 2300 Chestnut Street, Suite 200, Philadelphia, PA 19103, or
call (800) 810-4145, ext. 5000, or e-mail special.markets@perseusbooks.com.

ISBN 978-0-7624-4344-4

Library of Congress Control Number: 2012937688

E-book ISBN 978-0-7624-4702-2

9   8   7   6   5   4   3   2   1
Digit on the right indicates the number of this printing

Designed by Frances J. Soo Ping Chow
Edited by Lisa Cheng
Typography: Baskerville, Bodoni, Helvetica, LL Record, Swingdancer,
The Only Exception, Times New Roman, and Trixie
Photo credits: Girl: ©Shutterstock/YuriyZhuravov; Concert crowd:
©iStockphoto/Robert Kohlhuber; Singer: ©iStockphoto/Shaun Lombard

Published by Running Press Kids
An Imprint of Running Press Book Publishers
A Member of the Perseus Books Group
2300 Chestnut Street
Philadelphia, PA 19103–4371

Visit us on the web!
www.runningpress.com

Lyrics for "Love You Like a Love Song" courtesy of Antonina Armato and Adam
Schmalholz (Downtown Music/DMS), and Tim James (Universal Music Publishing).

Lyrics for "The Big Bang" courtesy of Antonina Armato (Downtown Music/DMS),
Tim James (Universal Music Publishing) and Jimmy Messner (Warner Chappell).

I love you like a love song, baby. . . .

—Selena Gomez

Preface

The moment she shuffled through the hotel's revolving door, the pack of paparazzi converged on the pony-tailed teenager like she was a celebrity. Which, suddenly, she was.

"JOSIE! . . . JOSIE! . . . JOSIE!"

Short. Tall. Fat. Skinny. Light. Dark. Young. Old. All guys. All pointing cameras at her. All shouting.

"JOSIE! . . . JOSIE! . . . WHY'D YOU DO IT?"

Josie Brant only had to walk about twenty feet to the SUV, but it felt like a marathon being run barefoot on jagged rocks, every step more uncomfortable than the next.

The security guard tried to clear a path on the sidewalk, only to have it collapse into a thicket of camera flashes.

"WHERE'S PETER?"

Peter: that word once filled her with so much warmth, comfort, and inspiration. Now his name weakened her legs and pinched her stomach so tightly she could just barf.

A nervous rash formed on her chest, matching the clown-like circles that grew bigger on her cheeks with every dizzying wheeze.

Ugh. #SoNotWinning.

The massive buzzkill that was this oven-hot morning was as real as the heartbreak that crackled inside her chest. As real as the tear-smudged eye shadow that formed raccoon rings around her eyes. As real as the love songs she'd recently been so inspired to write. Now, she wished she could delete every damn memory. Forever.

"ARE THE RUMORS TRUE?"

Ten more feet.

With every flash, she imagined what story their pics might tell. Would she look like a fourteen-year-old small-town girl caught in a bad celeb romance, or just another cheap looking groupie in a short skirt and black boots?

If only she had a baseball cap. Then she could slide it down low and hide her face. But Josie had left her tomboy hats—not to mention her anonymity—back home in Bakersfield. And home had never felt so far away.

"Josie," a chubby journalist with a British accent pressed. "Are you really a fame whore?"

Disgusted, she wrinkled her face and kept walking faster, inciting an elbow-to-elbow photographer frenzy that caused one guy to knock his bulky camera lens into Josie's forehead. A line of blood trickled down her cheek as if in a race with her tears.

For as long as Josie could remember, songs played in her head—even amid the chaos of her life. Especially amid the chaos of her life.

> *Silence can come when I die*
> *But till then I will speak*
> *Not a single lie. . . .*

The British reporter pushed closer, so close in fact she could smell his coffee breath. As she stepped into the SUV, the man asked, "So what is the truth, Ms. Brant?"

The crowd stood silent. Josie turned to face them. She inhaled and closed her eyes.

"The truth is," Josie said, exhaling. "The truth is, I was just a fan."

1

"**Oh, crap,**" Josie said. "My mom's writing on my wall again."

Josie scrolled her finger across her phone screen and shook her head. "So embarrassing."

"Now what?" Christopher asked.

"That pic of you and me at lunch today I posted," Josie explained. "You know, the one where we're flashing peace signs? She just 'liked' it."

As usual, Josie and Christopher were making their postschool Starbucks run. As usual, Josie tooled on her phone, a white earbud stuffed in her right ear listening to music, her left ear open for conversation. And, as usual, they waited for Josie's always-late BFF Ashley to join them. Not that Josie didn't mind some quality one-on-one time with Christopher. He was her "Boy BFF," after all. Or as she affectionately called him, her "BBFF."

Christopher squirmed in the puffy leather chair and reached for her phone, adjusting his black-frame glasses and glancing at the message. "Lemme see that. . . . Oh, nooooo."

"Oh, no, what?" Josie plucked out her earbud.

"Your mom's comment. She wrote 'LOL.' Like, who writes 'LOL' anymore?"

Josie snatched the phone back. "Um, geezer stalkers like my mom do?"

"Josie, I don't think thirty-eight years old puts her smack in the middle of Geezerville. I mean, Sheryl Crow is way older than your mom—she's still totally cool. And hot."

Josie put the phone down on the table. "Okay, fine. But A, you have a MILF crush on Sheryl Crow, and B, my mom is totes stalking me."

Christopher laughed. "Uh, yeah, true."

Josie's brown eyes popped wide open.

"What?" Christopher asked.

"She added a wink-face." Josie sighed. "Moms should not wink-face anybody. Ever. So 2005."

Just then, her phone buzzed to life with another text alert.

> Sorry, joseski. runnin late. Eddie is hittin on me BIG time at cheerleading! bahahaha. C u in like 5.

Ashley. Josie tapped her back a message, her fingernails sounding out a rat-a-tat-tat rhythm on the touch screen.

> Kk lil miss tardy pants. dont forget tho . . . need to get ready for the big PM concert 2nite

> obvi! Duh. Will pick ya up with my mom ASAP

"Let me guess . . . ," Christopher sneered. "Blondie?"

"Yep."

"And let me guess: Eddie's hitting on her."

"Wait," Josie replied. "How'd you know that?"

"Because Eddie just texted *me* that he's quote-unquote 'throwing the mack down' on Ashley. Ahh, kids these days." Christopher sighed.

"Yeah, silly kids." Josie giggled. "Silly, silly, silly kids."

"Those gosh-darn *screen-agers*," Christopher Southern-drawled. "That there *Intra*-net is ruinin' the youth of America!"

Being a year older and a lot smarter than every other boy she knew at Bakersfield's Lawndale High, Josie's BBFF carried a sense of maturity, and humor, that made Josie feel, by osmosis, a little older and more clever herself.

"Speaking of silly kids," Christopher continued. "What time's your *silly* concert tonight?"

"Um, eight, I think," Josie said, pretending she didn't know the exact time her guilty celebrity pleasure would be taking the stage downtown at Rabobank Arena. "You sure you don't wanna come?"

"No *gracias*. Not my cup o' tea. Not my slice of baloney. Not my—"

"Okay already—I get it!" Josie cupped her hand over his mouth. "You don't like Peter Maxx. Whatever."

Christopher pried her hand from his mouth and sipped the last vestiges of his iced mocha through a green straw, gurgling it to empty.

"Josie," he said soberly. "Remind me again: Why do you like Peter Maxx so much? That is, remind me without mentioning his abs or his hair or his Chiclets-white teeth."

Josie's eyes lit up. "Do I detect a little jealousy, Mr. Evans?"

"Yeah, you got me." He raised his arms over his head like a captured bank robber. "My secret fantasy is to be a teen pop star. Shhh. Please, please, please don't tell anyone!"

"Well, Mr. Evans, you are the one who just told me that you're gonna be taking guitar lessons this summer."

"Correct. I'm taking lessons so that I can play obscure Chris Isaak tunes that no one has ever heard of—not so I can sell action figures and lunch boxes with my face on it to hormonal teenage girls."

"Just sayin' . . . ," Josie teased.

"Okay. Fine. Then how about this: *you* just told me that *you* are babysitting all summer, which can only mean you must want to join the cast of *Teen Mom*."

"Um, like, that would require me actually doing *it*." Josie fashioned her fingers into air quotes. "And, since it would require me having an actual boyfriend, that ain't happenin' any time soon."

"Please," Christopher said. "You could have a million boyfriends if you wanted."

"Not true."

"Totally true," he insisted. "Every guy in drama has a crush on you. Every guy in math has a crush on you. If you ever took your earbuds out of that little skull of yours, maybe you would notice."

"Yeah, yeah." Josie lifted her tank top and rubbed her belly. "But I would make a pretty hot mom, don'tchathink?"

Christopher smiled and rolled his eyes.

"Hey, speaking of hot moms . . ." With his pimple-spotted chin, Christopher pointed in the direction of the parking lot at a lady with big blond hair pulling up in a shiny black SUV. "There is Mrs. Cougarville herself."

"Eww." Josie looked out the window. "Okay, pervy Mr. MILF."

Josie stood up and stuffed her phone into the back pocket of her cut-off denim shorts. "Later, BBFF." She high-fived Christopher and hustled off with a flirty wave.

"Have fun with your *boyfriend* tonight," Christopher teased.

Josie plopped onto the backseat of the Mercedes and studied Mrs. Rogers. She wore an expensive full-length floral summer dress. Josie peered under the steering wheel at her wedge sandals, which revealed ten perfectly pedicured toes painted bright red. The diamond ring on her left ring finger rested on the leather-wrapped steering wheel like an ice cube. Josie could only see the right side of Ashley's mom's face, a smooth cheek that had a wrinkle-free texture that apparently had come after some expensive surgery. Ashley's father was Bakersfield's top plastic surgeon, after all. Plus, all the ladies who lived at the Las Palmas Hills Country Club looked like they belonged better in Beverly Hills.

"How's your mom doing, Josie?" Ashley's mother asked.

"Good. You know, still working at the hospital and stuff."

"Oh, that's great to hear. What with the layoffs you're always hearing about. She's such a sweet lady."

Josie stared blankly out the window.

Silence.

"Ashley tells me you're still writing music?" Mrs. Rogers continued.

"Well, sort of. I don't really write music *per se*. I just write lyrics."

"Oh, good for you. That must be a great outlet, what with everything that's going on in your life. Very therapeutic."

"Mom," Ashley hushed under her breath. She clenched her teeth. "Please."

Josie pretended not to notice.

Ashley's mom steered the car into Josie's apartment complex, slowing down as a gaggle of elementary school kids ran across the street chasing a soccer ball.

"Well, tell your mom I said hello," she said, pulling up to the curb in front of Josie's apartment building.

"Thanks, Mrs. Rogers, I will." Josie stepped out of the car. "See y'all in a couple hours."

Josie turned around to wave good-bye, noticing that Ashley's mom, rather than looking at her, was studying her aging apartment building's cracked stucco siding. Again, Josie pretended not to notice.

Josie's preconcert preparation ritual began the moment she scurried up the outside stairs to the second-floor apartment she lived in with her little brother and mom.

Their apartment had three bedrooms and one bathroom that they all had to share. Their living room window view: the parking lot of a strip mall. But the $850-a-month rent was affordable enough with her mom's paycheck as an occupational therapist. Josie knew it wasn't the lamest complex in Bakersfield, but it wasn't the nicest either. It certainly wasn't nearly as plush as the four-bedroom McMansion in the gated community they lived in before the divorce, before her dad retired from pro hockey and decided he would rather live alone than stop drinking and hanging with his hockey buddies.

Josie slid off her shoes and dropped her backpack on the tile floor beside the mountain of her brother's stink-bombed high-tops and various women's sandals and shoes. Josie had recently become obsessed with comfortable slip-on TOMS canvas sneakers. Her goal was to amass one pair for every day of the school week. She had red, navy, black, and chocolate. For her fifteenth birthday, coming in less than two weeks, she'd already asked her mom for a pair of the stonewashed ones. That would make five. #Perf.

"Josie, is that you?" her mom called from the kitchen.

"No," Josie deadpanned. "It's the Kern River Killer."

"Very funny," her mom yelled through the wall from the kitchen. "I'll have to call the cops."

As Josie made her way down the hallway to her bedroom, her mom, predictably, asked, "So how was school, honey?"

"Good!" Josie cheerily replied with the sincerity of a used-car salesman.

Her mom followed her down the hallway.

"Did you see my message?" she asked. "The Facebook one."

"I did," Josie replied lazily, turning toward the stairs and adding an obnoxiously gleeful, "LOL!"

"That Christopher, such a cutie," her mom said. "Such a nice boy."

"Sorry, Mom," Josie said, rushing, "but I really gotta get ready for the concert."

Meanwhile, Josie's twelve-year-old brother, Connor, sat on the couch blowing up bad guys in his testosterone theater otherwise known as *Call of Duty*.

"Hey, Josie," Connor said as his sister breezed by.

"Hey, Conz." Glancing at the TV, Josie added, "Hmm. Still workin' on that Nobel Peace Prize?"

Connor's eyes stayed fixed on the carnage, sinking into the sofa as if his butt was stitched to the fabric.

"Wait, wait," he said. "I have a question for you."

"Quick. I'm in a hurry."

"I'm serious."

"Okay. Fine, what?" Josie cocked her hands on her hips. "Make it snappy. I only have an hour."

"Okay, well, uh, I was wondering if you'd heard what Lady Gaga's right leg said to her left leg." Connor's fingers were still in full-out spasm mode on his controller.

"Gee, I have, like, no clue." Josie arched her eyebrows with mock enthusiasm. "Please, please do tell!"

"Nothing. 'Cuz they're never together! HAHAHAHA!"

"Oh-my-God! That is sooo HIGH-larious!"

Josie made a "C" shape out of her right thumb and forefinger and put it up to her forehead. "Creeper," she sneered. Connor had already ADD'd his eyes back to the TV screen.

Once inside the comfort of her bedroom, Josie began to focus on her concert prep.

Josie wiggled out of her jeans and T-shirt, wrapped herself in a towel, and scurried down the hall to the bathroom. She liked to steam up the shower before stepping in. Since her mom could never in a million years afford a visit to an actual spa, this was Josie's low-budget way of pampering herself.

After a few minutes, a knock came at the door.

"I hope you're not running the water when you're not in the shower," her mom yelled.

"I *am* in the shower," Josie lied, just then stepping inside the stall.

"Thank you!" her mom shouted.

Ten minutes, a palm load of exfoliating body wash, and two hair-conditioning rinses later, Josie stood dripping on the bathroom rug. She reached for the mirror, wiped it clear, and began her postshower inspection.

Kind of like a driver passing by a car wreck, she couldn't help but scan her body every chance she got. Lately, her body's appearance seemed like a moving target—her top, bottom, middle, front, and back all changing shape and form on a seemingly daily basis.

On "good" days, Josie would see the high cheekbones on her pimple-free face, a narrow waist, and athletic legs sculpted from years spent doing laps at the Bakersfield Dolphins Swim

Club. On "fat" days, she wished she could undergo a *90210-*style makeover. As much as she was always told how "skinny" she was and thus hated thinking this way, she would stare at the tiny bulge in her lower belly and obsess over what she had eaten over the last few days. On these kind of self-critical days when she felt as bloated as a water balloon, Josie would catch herself fantasizing about having a flat stomach and a bigger chest like Ashley's.

Today, though, she was not having a "fat" day. She twisted, craned, and turned and poked and stared and, well, didn't think she looked all that bad, actually. A victory. #ThankGod 4SkinnyMirrors.

She hustled back to her bedroom and pressed play on her Peter Maxx playlist, pumping up the volume. In front of the mirror that leaned against the wall opposite her loft bed, she began brushing her hair.

PING!

Josie put down her brush and glanced at her phone.

Ur meetin me at 630?

Ashley.

Totes am, Josie texted back with thumb-busting rapidity.

Josie slid on a pair of her mom's spiked heels from the shoe pile and squeezed into a tight-fitting denim miniskirt, sucking in her stomach as she snapped it on. "I hate skirts," she growled, uncomfortably wiggling out of it and kicking the shoes off into the closet.

Still a tomboy at heart (even though she quit ice hockey and softball when she turned twelve), Josie changed into her favorite pair of blue skinny jeans, black TOMS, and a tight white T-shirt, on which was printed in giant pink letters: MUSIC IS MY BOYFRIEND. The only girlie-girl addition was her silver peace-sign earrings, plus the carefully applied red lipstick and smoky eyes and Peter Maxx's sweet-scented Dreamcatcher perfume she sprayed on her neck.

She had to make one last check of @PeterMaxxNow.

Nothing. No updates in the last twenty-four hours. In fact, his last Tweet was of a pic he took from the stage of a packed arena two days earlier in San Diego:

You're welcome, San Diego! #SoGrateful #BestFansEver

Josie checked the time on her phone. Six o'clock. Two more hours until showtime.

2

Bakersfield. Another city, another arena waiting to be packed with screaming fans—mostly female ones, of course. Sure, there was the usual spattering of man fans, but they were pretty much either just boyfriends dragged kicking and screaming, or "cool" dads wearing baggy blue jeans and untucked office shirts trying to make their daughters think they were hip to the cause.

But Peter Maxx stayed most focused on his core demo: teenage girls. They were the ones who downloaded his music, stalked him on the Web, bought his concert tickets, T-shirts, hats, pens, screensavers, ring tones, pillows, cell phone covers, bottles of perfume, hairbrushes—whatever commercial products his management team could dream up making money by selling to his devotees. So devoted, in fact, was his following that thousands of "Maxx-a-holics" held online "group therapy" in live chats. Peter may have been only sixteen, but he was wise enough to know that he'd be just another struggling singer posting YouTube videos without his dedicated fans.

That being said, the tour was fast becoming a blur. Last night, he was at the Staples Center in Los Angeles. The night before that, San Diego. Three nights earlier, Phoenix. The next day . . . he didn't even even know yet. Oakland, maybe? He couldn't keep track. It was all so hectic. But Peter's dad was touring with him all along the way, keeping him focused on the music, keeping him from burning out. He always taught Peter that great performers "focus on the moment, not the memory." So, being the good boy who listens to his daddy, on that night it would be all about Bakersfield's fans.

It was a forty-city North American tour, Peter's first as a headliner. At the start, just about everyone—his record label, his dad, the concert promoter, sponsors—worried that the tour wouldn't sell out. On top of the usual concerns over whether parents would foot the bill for their kids to get tickets, an article in *Billboard* had just posed the question with an ominous headline: "Will Digital Downloads Mark the End of the Live Music Era?" Well, the answer, for now at least, was no: from St. Petersburg to Seattle, Peter had sold out each and every show.

That June night in Bakersfield marked the halfway point, his twentieth stop on a tour that wouldn't end until late August. By all the usual industry indicators—ticket sales, corporate sponsors, merchandise revenue, downloads, radio spins—the tour had been a complete financial success. Peter Inc. was raking in nearly a half-million bucks every show. Peter's dad kept reminding Peter, "Assuming everything runs smoothly, you'll be set for life. But you can never assume. To do that is to make an *ass* out of *you* and *me*."

From the outside, it appeared that even though he wouldn't even turn seventeen for another four months, Peter was already living his dream:

- Five of the top ten most downloaded songs in the last year

- Star of a hit cable TV show loosely based on his life and career

- Two Grammys (Best New Artist and Song of the Year)

- A house on the sand in L.A.'s posh Manhattan Beach

- A Porsche convertible for his sixteenth birthday

On top of all this, hundreds of girls (most of them super-cute) had been hanging outside his hotel every night, at every stop, hoping to get a picture or get video with their idol that they could post on Facebook and be the envy of all their friends. This is all to say that Peter Maxx was living the teenage dream. Or so it appeared.

The day before his Bakersfield show, Peter woke up and began another hamster-wheel day:

6:00 A.M. Wake-up call at downtown L.A.'s Marriott hotel

6:15 A.M. Breakfast delivery: grande iced mocha latte and a fruit plate and shot of wheatgrass

6:30–8:00 A.M. Phone calls with radio stations. Stations will dial in and time for fan connection

8:00–11:00 A.M. Private home-school tutor session

11:00 A.M.–12:00 P.M. Workout in the hotel gym/meditate

12:00–1:00 P.M. Vocal exercises

1:00–2:00 P.M. Lunch, band/crew meeting

2:00–3:00 P.M. Media interviews, promotional appearance for charity at L.A. Live

3:00–5:00 P.M. Rest/meditate at hotel

5:00 P.M. Limo departs hotel to Staples Center

5:30–6:45 P.M. Makeup, wardrobe, vocal exercises

6:45–7:00 P.M. Soundcheck

7:00–7:15 P.M. Meet-and-greet with fans

8:00–10:00 P.M. Concert

12:00 A.M. Veg out watching late-night TV, surf Web, Facebook, etc.

A towel around his neck soaking up sweat, Peter and his bodyguard, Big Jim, hopped into the limo at the Staples Center underground loading dock after the show. As his black SUV rolled slowly up the ramp to the downtown L.A. street, where hundreds of fans had gathered, they began screaming. SCREAMING!

Through the tinted glass, the "rabids" (as Big Jim called them) couldn't see Peter, but he could see them. He saw adorable eight-year-old girls in concert tees that draped down to their knees; teen superfans in barely-there dresses, short-shorts, and push-up bras; overly excited moms wearing way too much makeup (and occasionally too much Botox); dads cutely holding hands of their wide-eyed little daughters. Some lined the sidewalk holding signs—I'M MAXX'D OUT! . . . MARRY ME, PETER? . . . WE'VE WAITED A LIFETIME.

Peter's cheeks began to curve upward with a smile. Then, suddenly his face froze.

He spotted a woman who had to be in her forties waving a cardboard sign on which she had scrawled, PETER, CAN I BE

YOUR MOM? Tears glistened in his eyes as he craned his neck while the SUV drove by the lady, but Peter wasn't a crier. Instead, he squeezed the tears back, put on his sunglasses, and hoped Big Jim wouldn't notice.

"You okay there, superstar?" Big Jim asked Peter in a drawl that lazily stretched out his words in only the way that Southerners do.

The two sat quietly for a minute as the SUV rolled beyond the bedlam. "Hey, buddy," Big Jim said. "I know it's not always easy bein' you. I see how hard you work every day. You can feel down. It's cool."

"Thanks, Jimbo. You da man."

In recent weeks, Peter had been feeling more like a rock 'n' roll robot than a rock 'n' roll star. Morning radio calls at 6:00 a.m. Nonstop promotional appearances. The doctor said it was a nagging, borderline case of laryngitis. Mean-spirited bloggers and haters, one of whom felt compelled to scrawl "G-A-Y" over every picture he ran of Peter. He had gone five months without a single day off from work. On top of that, there was the pressure of being *the* Peter Maxx, or, as *Rolling Stone* had recently dubbed him on its cover the month before, "Peter Perfect." He had been practicing his daily meditation to manage the stress, but the hectic schedule had exhausted him.

Yet nagging him was the belief, etched into his brain by his father, that pop stars with perfect teeth, perfect looks, adoring fans worldwide, and all the money in the world just weren't supposed to feel sad, they weren't supposed to get emotional while riding in limos before sold-out shows. "Let me guess what you're thinkin'," Big Jim ventured as he steered up to the hotel entrance.

"Okay, Criss Angel," Peter replied, staring out the window. "Go ahead. Read my mind."

"Well, first of all," Big Jim said with a sigh that seemed to blow straight from his sizeable Buddha belly. "I'd reckon you probably be missin' your momma."

⏮ ⏹ ⏭

Bobby Maxx was twenty-five years old when he was about to break out. He had cut a demo tape of songs he'd written himself and given it to his Nashville neighbor, a recording engineer who knew someone, who knew someone, who knew someone at a few record labels. He was working at a Jiffy Lube, changing oil filters by day. At night, he'd work on his music in his garage and, if lucky enough to get a gig, play some of the local bars. He had written hundreds of songs in his life, but on that demo tape was the only song that would matter. It was the song that would take Bobby Ray from being an average oil-change technician to a country pop icon. That song was "Laurel."

> *Got word today*
> *A little man's on the way*
> *One thing's for sure*
> *Things'll never be the same. . . .*

He wrote it the same day that he learned that his girlfriend, Laurel, was four months pregnant.

With an open heart
We lie by the lake
Reflections of us
And the life we'll make. . . .

Bobby knew what was the right thing to do. He would have to marry his high school sweetheart; he would have to grow up fast, even though he was just twenty-five and barely had two nickels to his name.

Don't know how it'll work
You and me, we created life
Laurel, honey, now be my wife. . . .

By the end of the year, Bobby and Laurel were married and Hill Country Records signed Bobby on the spot after hearing his demo tape. Six months later, it became the number-one most played song on country radio, and Bobby, just like that, was a household name. His hit enjoyed more radio plays than Reba, Garth, and Brooks & Dunn combined. Then the song was remixed for Top-40 radio by a pair of pop producers, who replaced the steel guitar with an electric, and the countrified rim shots with power pop snare beats. The week that pop remix was released it went number one and stayed there for a record eighteen weeks. Bobby and his wife and son had themselves a crossover hit, the gold standard for pop music.

But by the time Peter was four years old, Bobby's follow-up album flopped. The handsome Tennessee cowboy instantly went from a boy wonder to a one-hit wonder. The world tour that his management had planned to launch on the heels of the album's release was scrapped. As suddenly as he had risen to the top, he fell. Hard.

Just before his flop, the young couple had rented a house in Laurel Canyon, a woodsy neighborhood atop the Hollywood Hills, with winding S-curve streets. Laurel never liked driving them and, no matter how hard Bobby tried, she didn't like very much about L.A., except, that is, the year-round summer-like weather.

One Saturday afternoon, she kissed Bobby and Peter good-bye and went for a drive down the hill to get some groceries. As always, she pumped up the volume and blasted the radio. As always, she had a smile on her face. As always, she was gorgeous—her blond locks flowing in the breeze as she rolled down the hill. But this trip would not have the usual happy ending of returning home to her two guys.

COUNTRY STAR'S WIFE DIES IN CAR ACCIDENT

LOS ANGELES—Laurel Maxx, 28, the wife of country star Bobby Maxx, died in a car accident Saturday afternoon on a cliff-side road in L.A.'s Laurel Canyon neighborhood. Mrs. Maxx lost control of her 1995 Ford Bronco on a curve near Lookout Mountain Road. An L.A. County Sheriff's spokesman says it appears she had swerved to avoid hitting a coyote, causing her SUV to flip over and tumble down an embankment. Mrs.

```
Maxx is survived by her husband and
4-year-old son, Peter. Mr. Maxx's
publicist released this statement
late Saturday night: "Bobby thanks
his fans for all their love and con-
cern at this tragic time, but asks
that his family's privacy be
respected while they mourn the loss
of a dear wife, loving mother, and
Bobby's creative muse."
```

With the help of Peter's grandparents back in Nashville, Bobby would have to raise Peter as a single parent. The industry buzz was that Laurel's death had delivered a creative blow to Bobby. Then came the rumor he couldn't shake: that he had a drinking problem. Like a lot of celebrity gossip, there was a kernel of truth to the tabloid reports. His career never recovered, and Bobby Maxx become another piece of roadkill on the music biz highway.

Thirteen years after his wife's death, Bobby, now working full-time as his son's manager, viewed Peter's success as good karma coming back to his family for all the grief they had endured. But for Peter, this intense desire of his dad to redress past wrongs all meant one thing for him: pressure. To make his dad happy. To not disappoint his loyal fans. Even after all his success. Even while being adored by—and raking in—millions. Even in Bakersfield.

3

"Mom, I'm ready!"

"Here ya go." Josie's mom held out the keys to her Honda Civic.

"Very funny."

"What?" her mom asked.

"Um, I can't drive for like two years, duh."

"Oh, that's right!" She spanked her forehead with her palm. "I absolutely forgot, because you do look twenty with all that makeup on."

Josie rolled her eyes. "Mom, you could be, like, the new Chelsea Handler. Seriously, you are that funny."

"Nice kicks, LeBron," Connor, a self-appointed fashion king, chimed in with a devilish chuckle from his throne that was the couch.

"Hardy-har-har," Josie replied, before blowing her brother an air kiss.

A half hour later, her mom dropped off Josie downtown at the Rabobank Arena.

Josie hadn't taken two steps out of her mom's car when Ashley ran at her with arms wide open and screeched, "Besterz!!!!"

The perfumed pair jumped and hugged as they bounced up

and down, their signature BFF greeting. They called it "jugging."

Josie even had written a rap about it that they sang when feeling especially goofy.

> *We be tight*
> *Peas in a pod, we got might*
> *Need no huggin'*
> *'Cuz we be juggin'*
> *Woop, woop!*
> *Juggin'*
> *Woop, woop!*

With every "woop," they raised the roof with their hands over their heads, inviting a sea of curious stares from other fans on the sidewalk.

Less than two hours later, thumping drums and bass buzzed Josie's body from head to toe, vibrations so loud she couldn't hear herself think. Not that there was a whole lot of actual brain activity going on.

More than anything, Josie was feeling *emo.* Then again, make that *hormonal* over the singer about to come onstage, a guy who had written songs speaking directly to her heart, that communicated a truth so deep and touching that Josie had trouble conjuring a word to adequately describe the thoughts and feelings his songs ignited in her. Rapturous? Too religious. Tasty? Too culinary. Sexy? Not even. What she felt for Peter even had to be better than sex. Or so she assumed.

There was just something irresistible about Peter. He was more than a sixteen-year-old guy with a perfectly messy thatch of dark hair strumming a guitar and singing about his deepest feelings. He was the only guy in the History of Guys that made her straight-A-achieving brain seemingly contain all the intellectual power of a fried-egg sandwich.

The sold-out crowd was now chanting, "Peter, Peter, Peter . . ."

Josie, meanwhile, was a far less obvious worshiper at the Church of Peter.

The sight: lots of ponytails and bright lipstick.

The sound: screaming.

The smell: perfume and sweaty fangirls.

Josie looked at three girls across the aisle also standing in front of their floor seats. They had to be around college age, and were wearing black sports bras that showed off their flat bellies, on which each had painted red letters that, when lined up, showed the message: WE LUV U. Their tight denim shorts and shimmering microminis left little to the imagination.

"Embarrassing," Josie mumbled to Ashley, shaking her head. "So embarrassing. Don't these girls have any shame?"

Ashley was too busy screaming to hear.

Josie refused to chant his name. Instead, she scanned the crowd, grinding her teeth in anticipation of what she secretly hoped would be one of the coolest concerts of her life.

"Loosen up, old lady," Ashley insisted, before going back to yelping like a lapdog.

What Ashley sometimes lacked in demure maturity, she made up for with a ripped-from-a-fashion-blog personal style.

Ashley wore a tight denim miniskirt (even shorter than the one Josie had tried on—and promptly taken off—back home), a black cap-sleeve T-shirt with silver sequins stitched on the shoulders, and black heeled knee-high boots that made her seem five years older than she was. "When the lights go up, I'll sparkle," Ashley explained. "Seriously, besterz. Peter's so gonna see me!"

Unlike Josie, Ashley definitely wasn't afraid to fly her freaky fangirl flag. Fitted loosely on Ashley's wrist was a black rubber bracelet on which was printed in block white letters: PETER PERFECT. Josie was jealous that Ashley's parents spoiled her—Exhibit A being Ashley's $350 outfit and Exhibit B being the $200 VIP postshow meet-and-greet pass. Josie wished her parents could afford such luxury, but parental cash flow was not at all what it was before the divorce.

Josie kept her arms crossed and clutched her elbows, rolling her eyes and staring down the hormonal teen mob.

"C'mon, Miss Granny Panties!" Ashley shouted over the now ear-splitting screams. "This was supposed to be about having fun, remember?"

Ashley was a year older than Josie and was already planning her Sweet Sixteen party, which in just eight days she would host up at Camp Beaverbrook at Lake Isabella. She had invited ten of her best girlfriends for a two-day campout. Just about all of them were cheerleaders like her, except for Josie.

Josie's fifteenth birthday, however, wasn't for another eleven days, yet sometimes it seemed like she was the older of the two girls. Not so much because of the way Ashley looked, dressed, or even acted. Most guys, in fact, assumed that Ashley—more physically mature and always way more makeup-splashed—was older than Josie . . . until, that is, she began talking. *Like . . . ya know . . . ohmygod . . . totesy . . . duhhh.*

To her credit, though, Ashley was a fun girl. She was the one who infected Josie with the habit of making up playful news words for just about everything. It started as their BFF-speak shorthand to fit words into 140-character Tweets, but now it had taken over their real life vocab. Like, for example, Josie's name. To Ashley, Josie was "Jo." Precious was now "presh," delicious became "delish," super was "supes," and totally was now always said as "totes." Lately, the next step in the evolution of their BFF-speak was to add the suffix "-ski" to select words, meaning "totally" was now "toteski." It was annoying to pretty much everyone but them, which made them like it even more.

Normally, Josie loved Ashley for her goofiness. It was comic relief from her own life, which she, admittedly, sometimes took way too seriously. But, on nights like this, when Josie would rather just chill and enjoy a concert rather than gesticulate herself like a yakking bobble head, Ashley—with her perfect posture and detachment from reality—could get under her skin.

Josie had been friends with Ashley since the fourth grade, when they both were in swim club together. In fact, they began calling each other "BFF" before it became cool.

Over the years, both had changed a lot. Ashley got into cheerleading, while Josie became passionate about music and writing. Ashley got boy crazy and needed to be talking to at least five boys at any given time, while Josie had good guy friends and, while she had her crushes, she never had what she would even come close to calling someone a "boyfriend."

The only real mutual friends the girls shared anymore were Christopher and Eddie, a punk skater boy who had a crush on Ashley since seventh grade (still, they'd never kissed). None of Ashley's cheerleader girlfriends were very nice to Josie. But they had been "Best Friends Forever," and loyalty was something that meant a lot Josie, so the friendship remained.

One thing they enjoyed together: Peter Maxx.

Part of Josie (the rational part that thought the whole Peter-mania was a seriously colossal generational embarrassment) was already mortified enough just to be standing in front of her tenth row seat, waiting anxiously to start singing every line with every other biochemically overexcited girl from Bakersfield. But every girl has her guilty pleasures. And, for Josie, it just so happened to be Peter Maxx.

Josie liked to think of herself as an aberration from the norm, not some teen cliché queen. So, she just kept thinking, if she could at least wait to be so obviously into Peter until the arena fell dark, she'd consider the night a smashing success. Such was her state of being. As Britney Spears once sang: not a girl, not yet a woman.

Josie knew full well that every fangirl wants to think she has a special relationship with a singer, that she has thoughts and feelings that no one in the world could possibly understand, a connection so deep it's cosmic! But, when it came to her connection to music, and especially Peter Maxx's songs, she just believed that their connection was uniquely special. Josie felt dorky even thinking something so cheesy, let alone telling anyone—even Ashley—this crazy fantasy that she hid in her brain.

You couldn't tell by looking at Josie at that very moment—she on her tippy toes so as not to miss the moment Peter came onstage—but she really did have a valid claim at being a unique chick:

- ☑ She was one of the few girls at Lawndale High who didn't belong to a catty clique. Just Josie Brant: A+ student, D+ dater, and A+ free spirit.

- ☑ She was the only freshman taking an AP English class.

- ☑ With no boyfriend and no catfights on her record, for someone who technically was a drama club nerd, she lived a relatively drama-free life.

Yet here Josie stood on the floor of the arena with her expectant eyes glued to the strobe light–splashed stage.

Most boys her age were too busy popping ollies on their skateboard or trying to get to the next level in *Rock Band* or *Call of Duty*. Boys. Peter was a *guy*.

Josie's mom was okay with Josie's "little obsession." Her daughter didn't drink or do drugs, didn't obsess over boys to the point it hurt her grades, and she had never even puffed on a cigarette—not to mention done anything remotely illegal. Josie had kissed only two boys in her life. Not as prolific a record as Ashley (nine boys and counting), but who needs boys when your addiction is Peter Maxx, the greatest singer-songwriter of your generation, the best thing since God created Twitter?

But now Josie stood on the arena floor, wishing Christopher had come. Even Peter haters were converted to lovers after seeing him live. But Christopher stubbornly refused.

Even so, that didn't stop Josie from hyperactively texting Christopher a blow-by-blow account of everything from the arena floor as they waited for Peter to take the stage. Ashley noticed Josie's fingers texting furiously and told her, "You guys should totally be boyfriend-girlfriend. You guys are obsessed."

"Never," Josie replied. "Why ruin a perfect friendship by complicating everything?"

"Um, because you *love* him?"

"I do love him, but I am not *in love* with him."

"C'mon, Jo-Jo. You guys are like ten times more in love than any couple at school."

"Well, A, we're just friends, and B, Christopher doesn't like me like that anyway."

"Okaay," Ashley teased. "Denial isn't just a river in Africa. I'm just sayin' . . ."

"Sayin' what?"

"That you guys would be an awesome couple. That's all."

Ashley snatched Josie's phone from her hands and began scrolling through her most recent text chat with Christopher.

"Oh my god, Josie. You guys have texted each other like fifty messages in the last hour! You guys are ridic."

"And your point is . . ."

"If that isn't true love, I don't know what is."

Ashley handed the phone back to Josie and glanced at her sideways. "Are you sure you guys aren't doing it?" She giggled.

"Stop!!!" Josie begged, as she typed out another text to him. "I'm not 'doing it' with anyone!"

Ashley raised her left eyebrow in a skeptical arc.

"Ash, I'm not kidding. There's zero chemistry. I'm so not attracted to him like that. He's just a sweet guy. Don't worry. We're not sexually active. Just textually active."

Still, Ashley wouldn't let up. "Well, FYI: you're totally marrying him."

Josie, however, was attracted to Christopher's brain, not to him physically. First of all, she was an inch taller than him, and the fact that Christopher's dad was a tiny man of five-foot-eight meant he didn't have much upside potential in the height department. And when they hugged, she could feel the bones of his shoulders pressing against her. He didn't have the muscles or height of someone like, say, Peter Maxx.

She wasn't proud of herself for being so superficial, but this was just how she felt, though she would never tell Christopher this.

Who's always there when no one cares
Who's my Band-Aid when my feelings get cut
It's you, my best friend, my best man,
no one compares

Josie didn't pretend to know what being "in love" was anyway, having never been before, but all she knew was that the feelings she had for Christopher weren't the kind that she felt when, say, she saw Peter Maxx sing. Peter made her want to do more than, well, just kiss.

Recently, someone had asked Josie on her Formspring account, "What's your definition of being 'in love'?"

Josie thought long and hard about it. This was a topic she had spent many hours, if not years, pondering. And, naturally, she wrote over a hundred songs about this very subject by age fourteen.

An hour later, after careful consideration, she posted:

I would think that being in love means I am as passionate about a person as I am about music. But, even as I write this, I feel like that is a naïve definition. The truth is, I only know infatuation.

And infatuation is how she described the kinetic movement she felt with every tingle in her chest when she watched Peter Maxx sing.

Josie had never before felt like this about any celebrity. Actually, make that anyone—famous or not.

Peter Maxx was her first and only crush. Period.

Josie was a goner from the first day she saw a video of him singing his breakout ballad, "No Regrets."

You flew into my world
We took off like jets
No regrets. . . .

The pop song became the go-to slow dance at every high
school prom, not to mention Josie's freshman year anthem.

Make a wish
Take this kiss
Girl, I've waited a lifetime for this. . . .

Now the teen star had brought his sexy self to her home-
town of Bakersfield, California.

The sellout crowd of 10,225 started chanting twice as loud
as before. When Ashley noticed Josie still wasn't joining in, she
knocked her in the ribs with a peer-pressure elbow. "C'mon,
besterz!"

"Okay, fine," Josie relented, flashing a smile.

"PETER! PETER! PETER! PETER!"

4

Peter sat with his eyes closed listening to the crowd chant his name.

The headset-clad stage manager peeked his head through the half-open dressing room door. "Fifteen minute warning, Peter!" he announced.

"Okay, y'all clear out now," Bobby said pleasantly to the dozen or so roadies, dancers, band mates, and various crew ritualistically gathered in the cinderblock-walled locker room.

After the door closed, Peter unzipped the inside pocket of his messenger bag and pulled out a manila envelope and reached inside, grabbing hold of a Ziploc bag filled with photos. One by one—about a dozen in all—he pulled them out and laid them on the table. Each picture had one thing in common: they contained an image of his mother. Holding him as a baby. Helping him blow out the candles on his first birthday cake. Hugging him after he got his first guitar at age four.

Peter had stopped praying many years ago. Raised Baptist, his parents instilled in him solidly Christian values, but, as Peter got older, the idea of talking to God seemed kind of silly. From his perspective, no matter how hard he prayed, his mom would never come back. One day when he was thirteen and was asking God to send various messages to his mom, Peter had a revelation: Why not just speak directly to mom? *I don't need a middle man.*

Ever since, Peter pulled out the photos and talked softly to his mom, just as he was doing minutes before taking the stage in Bakersfield.

"Mom," he began. "I wish you were with us here. Dad's doing good. A little stressed lately. But good. He'll always love you, Mom. I don't think he will ever love anyone else again."

Peter felt calm for the first time that day.

"Yeah, things with Sandy . . . well, they're so-so. I think it's hard to find a girl these days who'll just take me for who I am. But, that's okay. I'm figuring it out."

Peter then unrolled a purple yoga mat and placed it on the cement floor. He sat on the mat and lay on his back. He lowered his eyelids across his eyes as if they were blankets. He placed his arms at his side, tilted his palms up, and inhaled through his nose, filling his lungs with so much air his chest stretched his T-shirt, then released it with a forceful, smooth exhale. He could feel the muscles around his eyes relax and the pinching in his gut dissipate. His head tingled as a result of the burst of oxygen into his system. Peter repeated the deep breathing for several minutes, until every muscle in his body had relaxed and his mind was still.

Ten minutes later, Peter, his breathing so subtle his chest barely rose, slowly wiggled his fingers, then his toes, then gently rolled onto his left side and took a final deep breath. Centered. Focused. Ready.

Knowing that thousands of fans awaited him, Peter stood up, kissed his forefinger, and touched the picture of his mom standing on the front porch of their old house in Tennessee. "Okay, gotta go, Mom. Love you."

Peter pulled the pictures down from the mirror and placed them inside the baggie, zipped it tight, and stuffed it back inside the envelope.

"Yo, Peter," Big Jim shouted through the door. "We ready?"

Peter had one last ritual to perform before taking the stage. He picked up his phone.

@PeterMaxxNow hey, Bakersfield. I can hear ya guys. Are we ready to do this?!

Fascinating what a message 140 characters or less could instantly do to a crowd of anxious fans. Every inch of the arena floor vibrated, even in the dressing room.

He looked in the mirror as the makeup lady dabbed some antishine powder on his forehead. The chorus of chanting fans echoed down the hall to his dressing room.

That sound never got old. It reminded him why all those morning wake-up calls and dog-and-pony radio station and shopping mall appearances were ultimately worth it. That sound also reminded him of his childhood, when the dream to become the world's next big singer-songwriter began.

PETER! PETER! PETER!

5

Write a great song, someone will record it. Market a great song, someone will buy it. But sing a great song, and someone will *feel* it.

As Peter stood under the bright lights at his silver-bedazzled microphone for the next two hours singing straight from his heart to the hearts of his fans, Josie was definitely feeling Peter Maxx.

Shortly after eight o'clock, when a guitar-carrying Peter finally walked onstage to eardrum-piercing screeching, Josie's first thought was that a bicep flex and stubble of chin hair never looked so hot. Her second thought: there was nowhere else in the world she'd rather be than right there. While other fans captured him on video with their phones, Josie closed her eyes and soaked in the moment.

She sang along to every song, having memorized the lyrics long ago, her voice growing hoarse. Sweat dripped down her cheeks. At one point, as Peter walked down the stage's front catwalk jutting into the crowd, Peter looked in her direction and cracked a smile.

Did he just look at me, Ash?

I think so.

Get out.

No, for realz!

#ICouldDie.

6

Lesson **#1** of pop superstardom: you can't please everyone.

One fan weighed in with a YouTube video of Peter and his girlfriend doing a duet near the end of the Bakersfield show:

> THERE'S ROMANCE AND THEN THERE'S SHOWMANCE. CLICK ON THIS VIDEO AND SEE THAT PHONY-BALONEY SANDY JONES (THE FAKE GF OF PETER MAXX) PERFORMING A DUET LAST NIGHT IN BAKERSFIELD. WARNING: YOU MAY WANT TO HAVE A BARF BAG HANDY!

Yes, *that* Sandy Jones: the blondest, perkiest member of the G Girls, the opening act for Peter's tour. Peter and Sandy (or "Pandy," as fan sites cheekily call them) began dating when G Girls made a guest appearance on Peter's hit TV show, *For Pete's Sake.*

The blogs charted the rise of Pandy in great detail. Speculation about the couple soon became a global teen obsession. A lot of the rumors weren't true, but what was an undisputed fact was that Peter met Sandy during a dark phase. He was three seasons into his TV show and had released two sugar-sweet pop albums. Even though he'd sold 3.2 million records, practically unheard of in the era of pirated downloads and iTunes, Peter was frustrated that his label wouldn't let him make the record he wanted to make: a *real* album—songs that dealt with love, loss, regret, dreams, secrets, heartbreak.

The low point came when the label forced him to change the opening line of his first single, "Be with You Again." The line he and his songwriting team had written originally was "I've got this tingling feeling deep inside," but the label made him change it to, "I've got this feeling that you could be mine."

"Dad, what's so offensive about that line?" Peter fumed. "I mean, is it *tingle*? You gotta be kidding me! Grampa's leg *tingles* when he falls asleep in the recliner! It is totally outrageous. I've done nothing but play by their rules ever since we came to L.A. I don't think I can do this anymore."

"Son, I hear ya, but . . ."

"Or is it the *deep inside* part? I mean, are they sickos? For real. They honestly think I'm writing porn or something?"

If it weren't for an iron-clad contract with Retro that essentially gave them total creative control, if it weren't for his dad reminding him how "lucky" he was just to have a recording contract at all, if it weren't for his fans pining for his new album, Peter would have quit right then and there. This was before he learned how to breathe through stressful situations.

Retro promised Peter that his next record, scheduled to drop after the end of his current tour (and just after his seventeenth birthday), would be creatively all his. They promised they wouldn't censor any mentions of sex—indirect or otherwise, that they would allow him to explore his artistry in a way that would appeal to an older audience. But the label insisted he'd have to tour his current album. Or, as the label president bluntly described it to Peter's dad when they hand-shook on the deal, "Market the piss out of it."

Fine. Peter decided he could live with that. Though it wasn't exactly inspiring language.

But he still wasn't psyched that he had to promote his current record, which featured twelve songs, five of which he just plain didn't like and was forced to record. In fact, if Peter ever refused to record a song they wanted, his lawyers told him they could sue him for breach of contract. "That's show business, son," his dad told him. "You do your *business*, and they *show* you the money."

Peter appreciated everything his father did for him, despite his knack for Donald Trump–isms and for his "the-end-justifies-the-means" attitude. His dad's heart may have been in the right place, but it just so happened to be in the same place as his wallet.

Sandy wasn't offering much of a sympathetic ear. Whenever Peter offered the smallest complaint, she was always quick to remind him, "Shine—don't whine." Peter figured she got most of her rhyming one-liners from self-help books, but he'd never asked. He just knew that for a seventeen-year-old girl who dropped out of high school last year to join the G Girls, she sure had an impressive arsenal of motivational words at her disposal.

Before heading out on tour, Peter and Sandy walked their first red carpet together at a friend's movie premiere. Until then, the couple had only been photographed by paparazzi— shots of them leaving restaurants, walking at the mall, walking along the surf in front of his house in Manhattan Beach. But they had not yet "posed" at an official red carpet event.

On the carpet, Peter could barely muster a smile, but Sandy was all pearly whites and well-rehearsed posing (right down to the classic one-hand-on-the-hip "triangle"-shaped modeling pose).

When it came time then to do interviews, she grabbed Peter's hand and hightailed it to the press line. She was outgoing, funny, a goofball, her mouth going a mile a minute. Everything Peter was not. But he liked letting someone else have control for a change. It took the pressure off.

Sandy loved to talk about herself. Peter, however, was shy, slow to get to know, and was known in journalism circles as "a bad interview"—lots of one-word answers, a fair amount of mumbling, and a reluctance to share too much information about his personal life. "I like to keep that for my music," he explained every time a reporter asked a question that was too personal . . . "Are you in love?" . . . "Will you guys get married?" . . . "Where was your first kiss?" Pure torture. As much as Peter loved being a singer, he hated being a celebrity.

Right after their red carpet debut, an influential blogger called him "moody," and almost immediately Retro Records hired a so-called "media trainer" to teach him how to be more so-called "media friendly." When the trainer told Peter he had to start by smiling more, Peter told him he didn't want a job that made him pretend to be happy when he wasn't. The label backed off.

Even though Peter was not always a Happy Harry, he was a whole lot sunnier than before he met Sandy. Many fans saw things differently. They were divided between "Team Pandy" and the hate-a-holics who just couldn't stand the girl group star.

Take, for example, this comments-section debate beneath an OMC blog posting about Sandy and Peter hanging out at the beach:

> April 21 @ 1:26 p.m.
> *lovesIt* said:
> She needs to stop being a user bitch. She thinks she's so hot in that bikini. Seriously.
>
> April 21 @ 01:27 p.m.
> *girlygal* said:
> Agree. Sandy is a user. Lame. Y's he even with her?
>
> April 21 @ 01:29 p.m.
> *IluvMaxx* said:
> Because she's BLOND and has big BOOBS. Duh!
>
> April 21 @ 1:33 p.m.
> *TeamPandy* said:
> All haters need to chill. Sandy makes Peter happy. That's all that matters. Every1 CHILL!

But from the moment Sandy walked onto the TV show set, she brought Peter out of his funk. After the table reading of the script for the G Girls' episode of his show (in which the girl group plays his high school prom and Peter's character falls in love with her), Sandy came up to Peter and playfully said, "Hey, mister. You didn't smile once the whole time."

"That's because the script is kinda lame."

"You know what you need?"

"Better writers?"

"No, silly," she replied with a punch to his upper arm. "A trip to Baker's Bread! They've got *the* best mac and cheese. Let's go."

She made him laugh and was extremely cute, and at the end of his staccato chuckle, he realized it was the first time he had genuinely laughed in weeks. They drove together to North Hollywood to Baker's for lunch, their first date, and hadn't stopped dating since. They were, so far, an "everything but" couple. Sandy had been pushing for sex, but Peter wanted to wait. "You're probably the first guy in the history of guys whose girlfriend wants to have sex and you don't," Sandy pestered him.

It's not like Peter didn't *want* to have sex. He just wasn't sure if he really wanted to do it with Sandy, wasn't sure if he was in love with her. He had made that mistake with his last girlfriend—and when they had broken up, it had only made things harder.

It had taken him almost a year to figure out his confused feelings about his girlfriend. Yet, since paparazzi followed him practically everywhere he went, it wasn't long before the entire Peter Maxx fandom felt as if they knew everything about Sandy and Peter.

Everything, that is, but the truth.

7

PING!

Josie snapped awake and sat up straight.

Josie, where r u? duh!

Oh, no. Ashley. 7:34 a.m. and Josie and her mom were supposed to pick her up at 7:30 so they could get to school by 7:52, the latest they could walk into first period without being marked "tardy" and assigned to detention hall that afternoon.

Forgot 2 set alarm. Sorryz ☹ . . . b right over.

Josie had forgotten to tell her mom she needed a ride to school. The good news: Josie's neighbor, Delilah, was a senior and drove a 2005 Honda beater to school every day. Delilah served as backup transportation for when she missed the bus or her mom had already left for work because, on Fridays, her mom went in early so she could get out early and drive the hour down to L.A. to see her boyfriend, Thomas. She was relieved that her mom was finally moving on from the divorce; after two years of kissing frogs she had found someone she loved and who loved her (even if he was a nerdy accountant). But it was doing nothing for her ability to get to school on time.

Seeing her hair was a mess, Josie put on a purple baseball hat with a pink heart logo on the front. She ran out of the apartment just in time to catch the attention of Delilah, who was backing out of her parking spot.

"D!" Josie shouted over the muffler rumble as she ran toward the car. "D!"

D rolled down the window.

"What up, Brant?"

"Could I catch a ride with you?"

"Why? Where's your mom?"

"Work."

"Oh, that sucks."

"Yeah."

Delilah looked at the time on her phone. 7:42 a.m.

"Okay, whatevs. Hop in."

Josie plopped into the passenger's seat. "Is it okay if we pick up my friend? It's on the way."

"Who?"

"She's a sophomore," Josie said tensely.

"Don't tell me it's that cheerleader chick who's always at your apartment." D's face twisted into a sourpuss. "That girl is whiter than a roll of toilet paper."

"Ashley?"

"Don't know her name. But, yeah, she looks like an Ashley."

"Well, actually, yeah, Ashley is her name. But she's really not lame at all. She's pretty cool."

D thought for a few seconds, and then declared, "There's no such thing as a cool cheerleader." D looked at the time on the dashboard clock. 7:43 a.m.

"All right. Whatevs. Let's go."

D threw the transmission into drive and peeled out of their apartment complex and headed south on Gosford Avenue for about a half mile. She swerved right into the Oaks, one of the dozens of upper middle-class subdivisions spread around Bakersfield. When Delilah banked a hard right onto Ashley's street, the wheels squealed into the morning air.

"Whoa!" Josie said, her right shoulder pressing against the door frame.

But D howled like she was doing loops on a rollercoaster.

"The tires only squeal 'cuz they're bald," Delilah explained with an almost maniacal laugh. "No worries—unless the road's wet. Then we'd be in the ditches like bitches."

Luckily, Josie thought, it hadn't rained recently.

Ashley stood in waiting at the end of her driveway, a drab-blue book bag on her shoulder matching the bummed-out look on her face when she saw the black Honda streaking toward a stop in front of her.

"Jeesh, Josie." Ashley plopped into the backseat. "You weren't out *that* late last night! I mean, I'm the one who should be tired. I was out way later than you."

D shook her head in disgust and wiped her tongue across her purple lipstick-caked lips, as if she was mustering every ounce of energy in her body not to haul off on the perky cheerleader in her backseat.

"Sorry," Josie said. "Speaking of late, did you make it to Peter's hotel after?"

Ashley hesitated.

"Well?" Josie pressed. "Tell me!"

"When we get to school. I will. Don't worry. No big deal."

The car screeched to a stop at a red light. 7:49 a.m.

"Okay, okay. Seriously, sorry I'm late," Josie said. "I hate being late, but I had trouble falling asleep last night after the concert."

"What concert?" D asked.

"Peter Maxx," Ashley replied instantly.

Josie cringed as D burst into laughter and let out a noise from her throat that could only be described as a wrenching sound of disgust. "Oh, man, you guys. I can't believe you guys went to that lame-ass concert."

Ashley checked the time on her phone and exhaled nervously to no one in particular.

Josie definitely wasn't about to share the real reason she couldn't fall asleep: because she was so inspired by Peter's concert that she stayed up writing at her keyboard all night. As a matter of fact, it was a rush of creativity she hadn't experienced in a very long time, and she wrote an entire song.

She had already gotten into her shorts and a T-shirt, wiped off her makeup and was brushing her teeth when, just before midnight, the opening verse came to her out of nowhere.

I could craft a song with a catchy rhyme
But words can't describe your committed crime
You've stolen mine

She spat out her toothpaste and ran to her notebook that almost always could be found resting on her bed like a second pillow.

Texting hi, just because
That'll never happen
'Cuz we never was
Just twenty yards away you play
You might as well be miles away

She sat at her desk and turned on her Casio keyboard. And as she worked out a singsong melody in C, it was no longer a ballad, as she had hummed in the bathroom mirror. Instead, it was fast and it rocked.

Feeling what I've only heard for so long
There's no sad, just glad
No crime, but a gift
Each strum, each note a lift

D squeezed into a spot in the very back of the parking lot at exactly 7:51 a.m. "C'mon, Ash," Josie prodded. "At least give me a little hint. Did you meet Peter or not?"

"Yes."

"So tell me!"

"When we get to class. It's a long story."

Josie's friendship with Ashley often treaded the fragile border between love and hate, between mutual admiration and profound jealousy, between being true friends and being, well, frenemies.

The BFFs did have a storied history of on-and-off conflict, going back to the infamous *The Wiz* debacle, during auditions for the lead role of Dorothy (who wants to play a witch or a troll?).

Ashley ended up getting the part. Ashley, objectively, was a great singer. She had serious pipes. Ever since she was a little kid, her parents had her in church choir, taking vocal lessons, grooming her to be a vocalist. Ashley, Josie believed, deserved to get the role and, while the two friends occasionally engaged in healthy competition with each other, Josie acknowledged that if she couldn't stand up long enough to sing one song in a rehearsal, she probably wouldn't make a very good Dorothy when the theatre was full, the lights were bright, and that scary-ass twister was coming.

Instead, she decided then and there to focus exclusively on writing songs and became Ashley's biggest fan, happy to sing from the pit, or to pop onstage as a background performer. Just as well. Writing songs, after all, was her first passion.

As Josie sat on her bed after Peter's concert, she flipped through one of her old, tattered notebooks. Just reading lyrics conjured the emotions she felt at the time.

Angry . . .

> Who claims you can't come in first
> Like that
> Who claims you can't rhyme a verse

Like that
A fool who makes a claim
Like that
Is nothing but jealous and lame
Like that

Sentimental . . .

Teddy bear hugs
Imaginary bedbugs
Bedtime stories and eyelash kisses
Missing my life before boys and
*   high school disses*

Lonely . . .

Plotting a plan to make yourself cool
Eating fried dough and
*   blowing off school*
If this is what it means to be a teen
Throw me into a nerdy time machine

As lonely as she could feel at times, Josie thought everyone else spent way too much time wondering what group they fit into—the drama kids, the band geeks, the jocks, the cheerleaders, the stoners, the math nerds, the punks, the bro hos. She was perfectly happy in her own clique: songwriter.

Her parents never could explain where this unusual talent came from, but she'd had it since the first grade. Her mom didn't play an instrument, didn't sing, and generally didn't listen to music. And while her dad had self-taught himself piano and as a result could play a little keyboard, he had never actually written a song in his life. The closest thing to a song Josie even knew about was when her dad penned a poem to her mom that he had written on a napkin the night of their first date. *Kimberly, you're a babe that boggles/I swear I don't have beer goggles.* Not exactly a romantic sonnet, but cute enough that some twenty years later Josie's mom, even though now divorced, still hadn't found the heart to throw it out.

The morning after the Peter concert, Josie, wearing one of her "freakish" outfits the mean girls whispered about—TOMS shoes, skinny jeans, and a black Rolling Stones T-shirt—thanked D for the ride to school. Then she and Ashley plopped into their first period seats for Human Biology class and opened their books to the section on adolescent psychology.

"The human brain," Mr. Rickell began, "is not fully developed until into one's twenties."

The class giggled. Seated beside each other, Josie and Ashley smiled.

"Believe it or not, that wasn't meant as a joke," the gray-haired teacher continued. "The reason I tell you this is because, today, we'll be talking about adolescent sexuality."

More giggles.

"And before you can understand what you are going through, it's best to first understand that your brain isn't designed to fully understand what you're going through. In fact, the brain, especially abstract reasoning that is used to assess long-term risk and consequences, isn't fully developed until your early twenties. You may think you know everything, but biology tells us that you don't."

Mr. Rickell showed a slide from his laptop on the projector screen, on which appeared in giant block letters: SEX & ROMANCE.

"The difference is that one is an act, and the other is a thought," he said. "There's a reason why so much of art—our paintings, our music, our poetry, our literature—grapples with these two words more than any others."

The class fell silent.

"Sex and romance," the teacher continued. "On their own, each is confusing enough. But understanding and experiencing both of them at the same time, well, that is one of life's great challenges. You may live your whole life without entirely fig-uring it out. Hopefully this class will help you on your path to self-discovery."

Josie listened. But she didn't hear anything. She was too distracted by the sound of Peter's voice inside her head.

8

"**Fan relations.**" That's what Bobby Maxx called his son's acoustic sets at high schools, the countless radio interviews, charity benefits, mall shows, hour-long autograph sessions, and meet-and-greets before and after concerts.

"If you don't love the fans, then you don't love your music, because it has to be about the fans," Bobby reminded his sleep-deprived son in the limousine on their way to yet another appearance at a local Bakersfield high school.

As usual, Bobby was buzzing on a syrupy concoction he called a "red eye"—a monster cup of coffee with two shots of espresso, plus a spoonful of sugar dumped in, like some sort of bitter booster shot. Peter believed no man over forty should ever be that chipper that early, certainly not this far into a concert tour. As for Peter, he had a long night that even a heart-attack-in-a-cup couldn't fix. After the Bakersfield concert, he was up late arguing with Sandy at the hotel.

"I saw the way you looked at that girl," Sandy accused Peter the second he stepped foot inside the hotel after the pair fought through a mob of fans amassed outside the Bakersfield Marriott.

"What girl?" Peter asked, though he knew exactly what girl his girlfriend was talking about. "What are you talking about?"

"Um, the *hooker* in that tiny patch of denim she probably thinks is a skirt."

"Oh, okay. Got it. So now I can't even look at someone who's shouting my name in my face? Someone who, mind you, probably paid five hundred bucks for a meet-and-greet?"

Sandy grabbed Peter by the arm. "What I'm saying is that looking is one thing and *perving* is another." Sandy's cheeks glowed red. "You know what, though? I don't really care. She's just another loser groupie."

Peter didn't even try to pretend that he didn't check out Denim Skirt Girl. She was gorgeous and screaming at the top of her lungs, and, well, he assumed any guy would have at least peeked. But, if there is one thing Peter would take issue with, was what Sandy had just called his most loyal fans.

"Well," he snapped, "those supposed *loser* groupies are the reason we are even here, why we have jobs."

"Yeah, a job you complain about all the time," Sandy snapped, texting on her iPhone to avoid eye contact. "For someone who supposably loves his job soooo much, you sure do complain about it a lot."

"Supposedly," Peter corrected her.

Sandy looked up from her phone. "Supposedly what?"

"You said supposably. That's not a word. Supposedly is."

"Thanks, professor. Sorry, not everyone is Peter Perfect."

Peter stared down at the guitar pick he squeezed between his thumb and forefinger. The skin around his thumbnail was red and flaky, the detritus from a bad habit of biting his nails and fingers whenever he got too stressed. He had been trying to break the habit ever since last year. But it was proving a hard habit to break.

"Let's break up," Peter suddenly blurted. Peter looked as shocked when the words came out of his mouth as Sandy was. Like an unexpected burp, it gave him a sense of relief.

The next morning, Peter was thinking about what had gone down the night before. And he was not happy. Not happy that his girlfriend didn't embrace his fame, his fans, and just enjoy who he was. He was mad at himself for never solving his own problems because he was too busy trying to make everyone else in his life happy, so much so that he couldn't even tell the man sitting next to him the pain he felt.

Just then, his dad interrupted Peter's self-pity party.

"So here's the deal, Son." Bobby excitedly finger-scrolled his iPad. "Abby says no one knows we are showing up at the school today." Bobby knocked his son in the arm with his elbow. "I love it, I love it, I love it. This is gonna be a hoot!"

Bobby chuckled so hard that his long hair, graying at the temples, fell in front of his face. Brushing his bangs back, he added, "Dang it, you're gonna make this girl's year, Son." Bobby stomped his cowboy boot on the SUV's floor. "Plus, Hot Hollywood is gonna dedicate twenty-four hours of programming to you the day we release the new album. They're good media partners."

"Where are we going again?" Peter grumbled, grabbing the iPad from his dad.

From: Abby@prmusic.com

To: Bobby100@maxxinc.com

Hot Hollywood's Contest Winner Surprise Appearance

Peter will be appearing at Lawndale High School in Bakersfield on June 4. Limousine pickup at 8:35 a.m. I will meet you there. At 9:00 a.m. Peter will be surprising the winner of Hot Hollywood's "Sing It to the Maxx" contest. Jackson Phillips and his crew will meet you at the front entrance and will escort you inside. You will hand the winner a certificate to an all-expenses paid trip to see Peter in concert. Hot Hollywood will have all the winner information upon your arrival, but attached is a link of the winner's video. Will wrap at 9:30 a.m. and you will be driven directly to the airport.

"Dad, have you seen the video?" Peter asked.

"No, but Abby told me it's a good one. And she's pretty cute. Take a look."

Peter clicked on the contest winner's video submission. A pretty girl started singing a song she said she wrote just for him.

> *When you're just a kid and Mommy says good-bye*
> *You hug her, try not to cry*
> *Then Daddy wakes you in the night*
> *Says we gotta go, I don't know if she'll be all right*

"So this girl wrote this song herself?" Peter asked.

"Yep, well, that's what they tell me."

Bobby could see Peter's face twisting into knots.

"What's wrong, buddy?"

"Nothing."

"Son, c'mon. You can't fool the fooler."

"It's Sandy," Peter said.

As the car pulled into the school's parking lot, Bobby wrapped his arm around Peter. "We'll talk about it," he said, turning up the volume on the iPad.

> *Their angel's been taken, makes Daddy yell*
> *Please don't go . . . don't go . . . don't go*
> *Only God can rewind*
> *But I'm here to remind*
> *You before it's too late, or you're too old*
> *Kiss and hug and hold*
> *And sing your song*
> *'Cuz the trip ain't so long*
> *Breakin' hearts is always wrong*
> *Before you walk, please hear my song. . . .*

Peter stared out the window at the kids walking around the campus, their daily lives trudging along, lives moving on.

"Dad, I really want to cut this song."

"Mmm-k. We can make that happen."

"No, for real," Peter added. "I *need* to record this song."

9

"You did *not* get your picture with Peter Maxx," Josie declared. "No friggin' way."

"Sorry, but I did." Ashley giggled. "Swear. To. God."

As the pair walked out of first period, Josie was practically hyperventilating, kicking herself for not finding a way inside the meet-and-greet with Ashley after the show. But her mom wouldn't let her ride in someone's car past midnight, and she couldn't take that risk. Josie could have sworn Peter made eye contact with her in the crowd a few times, especially when he walked down the catwalk and strummed a guitar solo right in front of her during the second encore. She was just five rows away from him and, to Josie, it looked as if he—possibly maybe—cracked a smile.

But, still, she couldn't believe Ashley got to meet Peter Maxx! Plus, she got a picture with him. Not good at all. Sort of the story of her life: another missed boy opportunity. Just like the time when Frankie, her shy but cute neighbor, invited her to prom on Facebook. Stupidly, she didn't check her messages for a week. Result: she missed the dance. Or like when her dad gave her the option of spending last summer vacation with him in Canada, and she decided instead to stay home and be there for her little brother, since he got depressed when at home alone.

"So was he nice?" Josie asked.

"Ohmigod. So nice."

They plopped down on a patch of grass in the quad. "And, please, please, please don't hate me," Ashley added. "But check it out: he's even cuter up close. Perfect skin. Swearzy."

"I already am so hating you right now."

"Seriously, Jose-ski, don't get all hormonal on me."

The second-period bell sounded and the two girls grabbed their backpacks and walked across the courtyard. Their nerdy-but-nice musical director, Mr. Marrin, walked up as they approached class. "Good morning, ladies," he said with an emoticon-like smiley face. Mr. Marrin normally wore a tie and shirt to school. Today, he wore a brown corduroy sports jacket and a nice pair of jeans, the dress-up outfit he normally reserved for performances only.

"Ashley, can you come with me?" he said.

"Am I in trouble?"

"No, no, no. Just come with me."

"Can Josie come with?"

Mr. Marrin laughed. "Of course."

Josie noticed that not only was Mr. Marrin acting odd, but on most mornings the courtyard was bustling with kids hurrying to their next class. Instead a group of kids huddled on the far side of the courtyard by Mr. Riley's drama room, where Josie and Ashley had after-school chorus. The group of kids were trying to peek into the windows, but the blinds were drawn.

"Why's everyone freaking out over there?" Ashley asked.

"No clue," Josie replied.

She and Ashley stepped to the rear of the swelling mob. "Maybe ole Rilerz finally got in trouble with the principal for playing Eminem too loud or something," Ashley wondered.

"No. Really, Ash. This is so not normal."

They stepped through the crowd and into the classroom. Immediately, a TV camera pointed at them. Not like the kind of tiny flip cameras fans focused on Peter last night, or the cheap handy-cams they used in the AV department. Rather, it was a big news camera, with a light shining from atop it and an audio guy poking a boom mic at them.

"Surprise!" Hot Hollywood reporter Jackson Phillips yelled, jumping out from behind his camera guy.

If human jaws were physiologically capable of opening up so big that from a standing position a chin could touch the floor, Josie's and Ashley's would have done just that. The room full of students and some looky-loo teachers erupted in applause.

But as Jackson and the cameraman walked closer to Ashley and Josie, each girl's reactions looked startlingly different. Ashley beamed and put her hands to her oval mouth like a pageant queen. Josie, however, stood stiff as a mannequin, wrinkling her forehead in confusion the way one does when someone starts randomly speaking a completely foreign language to you on the street.

"Ashley Rogers," Jackson announced. "You've won the 'Sing It to the Maxx' contest!"

Josie's expression instantly turned into horror-film fright. But Ashley's "OH MY GOD" squeal redirected everyone's focus on the winner, who by now was jumping up and down as if on a pogo stick.

"Ashley," Jackson said. "Before we tell you what you've won, I'd like for you to meet someone. . . ."

The camera panned quickly to the person sitting behind the teacher's desk with his back to everyone. Slowly, he swiveled the chair around . . . "PETER MAXX!!!!!!"

Few moments happen in life when you experience something so jarring to your system that, just in order to comprehend what you're seeing, your brain, as some sort of primal coping mechanism, turns everything you're seeing into slow motion.

Peter's blue eyes filling up the room like light beams as he stood up and said, "Congratulations, Ashley."... Ashley darting toward the gorgeous pop star and hugging him ... the cameras capturing all the craziness ... the room, filled with a hundred or so people, cheering wildly ... Josie standing stiff as a statue ... her face turning white as the ivory keys on the piano keyboard she just wrote a song on for the guy standing right in front of her.

Confused. *Why is my best friend winning a contest? Why is Peter Maxx hugging Ashley and not me?*

Catatonic. The only part of her body moving was her eyes. Every other muscle, frozen.

Shocked.

Stunned.

Betrayed, again.

#SuchaBitch.

"Ashley, you beat out thousands of other contestants," Jackson announced as Peter placed his arm around the winner. "Your song moved the judges, including Peter. How do you feel?"

For a split second, Ashley looked at Josie across the room. Their eyes locked, but Ashley nervously looked away.

"Um, I feel like the luckiest girl in the world!"

Jackson Phillips tried his best to get her to answer a few more questions, but she was too emotional to answer. He instead turned to Peter and asked, "You've seen the video, Peter. What made her the winner?"

"The song. It's all about the song. Her lyrics touched me." Peter directed his gaze at Ashley, a fact not lost on Josie, who self-consciously slid off her baseball cap. She was having a bad hair day, but she didn't want Peter to think she was some tomboy softball girl. Josie fished a hair tie from her pocket and quickly fashioned a ponytail.

After Peter ended the interview, Peter asked Ashley, "Did we meet last night?"

Ashley tossed her blond hair over to the side, letting it flirtatiously dance on her left shoulder.

"Yeah!" she said excitedly, punching him playfully on his upper arm—almost too hard. "Oops, sorry."

"You've got nothing to be sorry about." Peter assured her with a pat on her upper back.

"Ah-hem." Bobby cleared his throat. "Tight schedule to keep."

"Sorry, girls, but we must be going," the publicist interrupted.

Josie leaned her back against the far wall of the room, overcome with that weak-in-the-knees feeling. The shrink who Josie's mom had made her see for a brief time after the divorce had diagnosed her with a psychological condition called Post Traumatic Stress Disorder—or PTSD for short. The divorce was so traumatic, the counselor explained, that certain "triggers" in her life made her feel like she was reliving that traumatic experience, sending her body into feeling as if it were in a state of "shock."

For, say, military war veterans traumatized by battle, a trigger might be the sound of the whooshing blades of a helicopter, taking them right back to a moment they feared for their lives. For a teenage girl who felt that her father had abandoned her and her once stable life was seemingly uncontrollable, a trigger could be something like a girlfriend doing something that made her feel like she couldn't trust her, that she might betray her on a moment's notice. And her body, in anticipation of the emotional assault, would go into shock mode: Weak knees. Sweaty palms. Heart palpitations. Dizziness. In other words, exactly what Josie was feeling in that classroom.

Not only had Ashley never mentioned she entered a singing contest, but she specifically had agreed with Josie that submitting a video for "Sing It to the Maxx" would be a "retarded" idea. "They probably don't even watch the videos," Ashley had said a few months back when Peter announced it on his fan page. "It's like a scheme to get you on an e-mail list or something."

As Peter's entourage began to scurry around him for an escort out of the room and into the quad, Jackson Phillips stuck his mic between Ashley and Peter.

"So, Ashley, what inspired you to write the song?"

"Well . . ." Ashley shrugged her shoulders. "I don't know. It's kind of complicated."

Josie's face began turning cherry red, her cheeks puffing like a blowfish.

"See?" Ashley began in a rush. "My best friend, Josie? Over there? It's her song. I just sang it. But she wrote it."

"Well, come on over!" Jackson Phillips said, motioning with his mic.

Josie wanted to walk up and say, "Celebrate what? Your thievery and deception and total betrayal?" But she didn't. Instead, she sheepishly shuffled forward, her feet heavy as bricks.

Peter extended his right hand, said, "Nice to meet you," and shook her hand. His large hand swallowed hers. His grip was firm but soft. Like a mattress you just want to sleep on forever. Their eyes locked.

As their hands stuck together, Peter's dad picked up his ringing cell phone. "Bobby here," he answered, stepping out.

If there ever was a time that Josie wished she wasn't a nervous palm sweater, that she wasn't a chicken, this was it. Peter, all six feet of him, stared right into her eyes for what seemed like forever. But, in fact, it was less than two seconds. Still, she had to look away. It was like staring at the sun.

Eyes so bright, stomach so tight
No words can describe your light

"Uh, nice to meet you, too," she said, pulling back her hand. Nonetheless, Peter gently squeezed it and pulled her toward him.

"Josie is a huge fan of yours," Ashley butted in. "Like, the hugest. For real. I couldn't have done it without her. She's a songwriter."

As Peter clutched her hand, her tension suddenly melted away—from her hand, then arm, shoulders, chest, stomach, legs, and feet. It was more soothing than any pill she'd ever taken, including the Xanax her shrink had given her for anxiety when she was thirteen and that she had quickly flushed down the toilet because it had made her want to puke and, worst of all, made her mind so mushy she couldn't write any songs.

Just when Josie, now squinting her eyes as if she had accidentally just seen her mom making out with her boyfriend or something, thought the overwhelming moment had ended, she felt two hands press against her back—one in the middle of her shoulder blades and the other, more memorably, on the small of her back. A boy had never touched her there like that. By the feel of the blood rushing into every part of her body, she definitely didn't want it to be the last time either.

Unsure how to react to his unexpectedly affectionate hug, Josie looked down at the floor, averting awkward eye contact. Her heart had been racing, but once he touched her back it was as if someone had injected her with Novocain. Her body no longer tingled, and for the first time since Ashley was crowned the "winner" two minutes ago, Josie could feel her feet touching the floor again.

Josie glared at Ashley, who shrugged a sorry.

Peter, oblivious to the drama unfolding before him, smiled as he gently released Josie's right hand.

"She's a great songwriter," Ashley told him. "I wanted this to be her surprise fifteenth birthday present. A secret present."

"Well, ladies, luckily there's no rule against singing someone else's song, as long as it is an original," Jackson explained. "You're still the winner, don't worry. Make that *winners*!"

As Ashley bounced up and down, Peter looked askance at Josie. He wrinkled his forehead in thought. "Wait a second," Peter said. "Were you also at my show last night?"

"Yeah."

"This might sound hard to believe, but I actually saw you. In that 'Music Is My Boyfriend' T-shirt, right?"

"Indeed."

Indeed? Oh, geez. What kind of dork says 'indeed'?

Peter laughed. "Definitely the best shirt I've seen on the tour."

Josie blushed and looked downward. "Thanks."

"So are you on Twitter?"

"Obviously."

"What's your name? I'll look for you."

Josie leaned in to him.

"MusicLuvr," she whispered.

Peter flashed a confused smile. He whispered back, "Music what?"

"Lover," she said, now full-on blushing.

Peter nodded. "Got it."

"But," she quickly added, "It is spelled L-U-V-R. Not L-O-V-E-R. That was taken, unfortunately." Josie laughed nervously.

"Okay, MusicLuvr." Peter patted her upper arm. "I'll look for your Tweets."

Before turning away, he gently brushed a strand of her hair back and tucked it behind her ear, combing it carefully with two fingers. A chill shot down Josie's neck and tingled into her back. "Bye," he told her. Josie could only stare back at him. Her body looked frozen, but it was on fire.

There's a difference between looking and seeing. *Looking* can only provide a two-dimensional glimpse of a person—an image you get from the pictures, the videos, the carefully crafted photo shoots, the interviews, the paparazzi images, the magazine covers, the impersonal Tweets. For Josie, seeing was definitely believing—that her connection might, just might, be real. At last night's concert, she felt him. Now she was *seeing* him.

10

All day long, the texts from Ashley came into Josie's phone. All day long, Josie didn't reply.

> How fun was that? Can u believe it? Hes soooo hot.
>
> Cant believe he hugged u!
>
> J, im so sorry I didn't tell u. I wud have but wanted to surprise u.
>
> Jose-ski . . . r u mad?
>
> Where r u????

The desperation oozed onto her phone all through Algebra II, Spanish, History, then AP English.

When the final bell rang at two thirty, Josie hustled quickly across the concrete-and-grass campus to her locker on the freshman row, looking over her shoulder nervously as she unlocked it and grabbed her backpack. *Friday. She must have cheerleader practice. Thank God.*

Josie put her head down and bolted for the back exit near the tennis courts, avoiding the front courtyard where most of the students hopped on buses or were picked up by parents.

"Josie!" a boy's voice called out from behind. She could tell it was Christopher, but she wasn't in the mood for anyone at the moment.

She turned around anyway, and saw Christopher running after her, his backpacking jostling awkwardly up and down. She flashed a quick peace sign, but nonetheless kept walking with purpose in the opposite direction.

"I heard what happened with Ashley," he said breathlessly catching up to her. "That's so messed up. Are you okay?"

"I'm fine. I'll text ya later. Promise."

"I'm here if you need anything. Psycho move on her part."

"Very psycho," Josie said as she made her way along the pathway toward a black pickup truck parked at the curb. The four-wheel-drive beast had dried mud splattered all over the sides and a windshield with so many dead bugs splattered on it they looked like they were sprayed on with a paint gun. Josie climbed up into the passenger's seat anyway.

"You really need to wash this thing," Josie said, settling in. "It's pretty disgusting."

The muscular man in a tight-fitting black T-shirt sitting behind the wheel nodded in agreement as he turned down the volume on the radio playing an old-time country song.

"Yeah, you're probably right," the man said. "It's dirtier than a pig pen."

He had unusually wide hands and thick forearms. His hair was dark, but for slightly graying sideburns, and it was buzzed short, revealing the outline of a receding hairline, the only part of his lean body that looked his age.

"So how was your day?"

Josie didn't respond.

"*Cómo estás?*" he said, his Spanish accent as authentic as a Taco Bell burrito.

"Dad." Josie exhaled. "If you really need to know, it was interesting."

"Interesting, good? Or interesting, bad?"

"Both."

Her dad turned left at the traffic light, heading west on Rosedale Highway toward the expanse of farmland that stretched out for thirty miles to the coastal mountain range.

"So, like, do you want the good news or the bad news first?" she asked.

Josie rolled her window down, hoping some fresh air would settle her down. When the pizza-oven hot air blasted her, however, she thought better and quickly rolled it up. "How about let's start with the bad," her dad said cheerily. "I like happy endings." Her dad hiccuped that redneck chuckle he reserved for his own jokes—especially the gross ones he knew would incite a reaction out of his daughter.

"That is so gross." Josie tried hard not to laugh. "Anyway . . . the bad news is that Ashley backstabbed me. But I don't wanna talk about it."

"Gotcha. Okay. Well, I'm glad you aren't bleeding on my seat. And the good news?"

"I got to meet Peter Maxx."

"Peter who?"

Josie laughed. The fact that her own father didn't know the name of her favorite singer reminded her how much they had grown apart over the last couple years. "The singer," she snapped. "You know, the pop star?"

Her father nodded and offered a cursory, "Oh, right," though he obviously had no clue.

"So what did Ashley do?"

"I said I don't wanna talk about it. Let's just say she's a bitch."

"Josie! You know I don't like it when you swear."

"Sorry, Mr. F Bomb."

"Seriously, Josie. Just 'cuz my truck is filthy doesn't mean your mouth has to be. Work with me."

They now were five miles west of the city, flanked on either side by a cotton field and a potato patch that stretched as far as the eye could see. This was Josie's ritual every other Friday night, an event she sarcastically had come to call "Daddy Duty."

As he drove them further outside of town and the strip malls gave way to farms, Josie noticed her dad kept looking in the rearview mirror every ten seconds. She turned back to see what the fuss was. She didn't see anything but a dark blue sedan tailing behind their truck.

"Not a cop, don't worry," Josie said.

"What's that?" he said.

"Yeah, the one you keep staring back at. It's not a cop. It's a Hyundai. Cops never drive those cars. You taught me that."

He gripped the wheel and stopped peering back in the mirror.

"So where's Connor?"

"His coach is dropping him off after baseball practice. So until then you get me all to yourself, lucky lady."

"Greeeeeat."

As part of the divorce settlement, Josie's mom got primary physical custody of the two kids but, per the agreement, they would spend every other weekend with their father during the school year; in the summer, they would spend half the time living with their dad. Her mom and dad sugarcoated the joint arrangement by telling them things like, "Now you will have two houses instead of just one!"

But, from the start, Josie wasn't sold on the new arrangement. Her mom's place was in the southwest side of town near the state college, and Josie could actually walk to stores or friends' houses. She could even walk to the movie theater whenever she had earned enough babysitting money to do so. Her dad, on the other hand, lived ten miles due west of the city limits, in a two-bedroom farmhouse wedged between a stinky onion field and spinach patch. Safe to say, Daddy Duty was not exactly a weekend in Malibu.

Connor had trouble understanding why their dad couldn't just come to their apartment for the weekend. "We aren't the ones getting divorced," he reasoned with maturity beyond his years. "Why should we be the ones to suffer?" Josie agreed, of course, but her mom and dad had sat her down and asked her to play Big Sister and help Connor accept the new arrangement, to sell him on something that she didn't herself want to buy. So she told her brother the truth.

"Definitely seen better days with work." Her dad broke the silence as Josie stared out the passenger window at the perfectly lined rows of crops angling off into the distance. "They cut my hours down. Economy's hurting everyone—just the way it is these days. But I've got some projects lined up. It's all good, hon. One door closes and another door . . ."

"Opens," she finished.

He smiled. "I taught you well."

As clumsy as her dad was in marriage (and car conversation), Josie never worried about him A, finding a girlfriend (at last check, he was currently dating three women, or, as he called it, "playing the field") and B, making money. Through his various hockey connections made by being a local sports legend, and his boyish charm, he always seemed to be able to find a way to pay the bills. The problem? He also found way too many ways to spend it: cars, boats, gadgets, family trips to a condo at Pismo Beach.

The pickup truck rolled to a stop in the gravel driveway in front of a Spanish-style farmhouse, a cloud of dust puffing up from the giant wheels.

When her dad moved into the house it was white, but blowing dust from the rectangular expanse of fields surrounding it had given the stucco a brownish hue. Her lungs, allergic to whatever it was that blew around the clay-rich fields, weren't the only victims of the dust clouds. "I got you some new pillows. I know you didn't like the old ones. And I have a little surprise."

Josie slung her backpack over her shoulder and followed him inside. The tiny living room and kitchen were tidy, but not clean. Obviously, her dad had tried to clean up quickly, probably by stuffing loose junk under the couch and into the closet. At least he was trying. Baby steps. Progress.

The old hardwood floorboards creaked as Josie walked into the bedroom. The room was bare but for two twin beds, one each for her and Connor, and an antique desk next to the window that looked out on a carrot field. This time of year, the lush green plants sprang from the dirt like organic pillows. By winter, after the harvest, the miles of farmland would turn to a sandy moonscape. A wooden swing hung from a thick branch of a lone oak tree by a thick but tattered rope. Josie stared at it and smiled. She had passed many long boring Saturday afternoons humming tunes as she swayed back and forth on it.

A mile down the road sat the Frito-Lay plant, from which wafted the scent of pretzels, corn chips, and potato chips at all times of the day. Her dad's house was almost always downwind from the plant. And while Josie had at first hated the greasy stench that soaked into her clothes by the end of the weekend, she had come to like it. At least it was something that reminded her of her dad when she went home for the week.

Josie unpacked the extra pair of shorts, sandals, a pair of Capris, underwear, and shirts she had stuffed in her backpack for the weekend. She pulled out her phone from the side pouch and saw she had four text messages since she left school.

Josie. Call me. Xo

I really wanna explain. Wud u just call/txt me?

Josie then checked her Twitter for Peter Maxx updates. She had hoped he would post a pic from his visit to Lawndale High. But nothing. She saw that a couple of friends had already uploaded stalker pics of Peter onto their Facebook pages, but nothing from Peter. Josie thought it was odd, as Peter normally gave daily fan updates to his social media sites.

Just then, a text message popped up from Christopher.

Hey amigo. Cheer up ☺

She typed a quick thanks back to Christopher but still kept Ashley on ice.

"Tit for tat?" Josie's dad said as he stepped into her room.

"Huh?"

"Knowing you, you're probably plotting how you can get back at Ashley."

Her father might have been out of touch when it came to knowing who her celebrity crush of the moment was, but she had to give him credit that he knew her personality inside and out.

"Let's just say, I'm considering all my options," Josie said with a smile.

"Want my advice?"

"Do I have choice in the matter?"

"Um, no," he responded. "Not really."

"Okay then."

"Take the high road, Josie."

"That's very noble of you, Sir Brant."

Josie went back to unpacking her clothes. She had forgotten to bring an extra tank top. She really needed to start leaving a set of clothes at her dad's house. She just never felt stable enough to commit to leaving anything. The unpacking, at least for the moment, gave her something to focus on other than her dad trying to lecture her.

"Trust me on this one," he continued. "I know you're pissed at Ashley, and I'm sure that girl deserves a little payback. But I'm serious. It's like when I played hockey. Whenever another player did something like chop my legs out from under me, or spear me in the gut, or cheap-shot me, well, nine times out of ten, I would react stupidly. So instead of the *other* team getting the penalty, I was the idiot who'd end up in the box. I was a hot head. I should have just skated off and not reacted. You know, taken the high road. Maybe if I did that more often I would have made it to the NHL."

"Life's not hockey, Dad."

"I used to think that too, but the older I get, the more I realize that hockey, basically, is no different than life."

Her dad stood by the bedroom door, his thumbs tucked into his jeans' front pockets. As he shifted his weight from one foot to the other, a loose plank under his right foot creaked.

He jumped slightly and looked out the window to the field behind the house.

"Did you hear that?" he asked.

"Hear what?"

He poked his head out the window frame and scanned to the left and right. "Ah, I don't know. Sounded like someone was back there. Must be hearing things in my old age."

"All righty, old man." Josie shut her drawer firmly with a clunk. "Thanks for the advice. Now what's for dinner?"

"I thought we could fire up the barbecue. I even picked up some veggie burgers for you. And whole-wheat buns."

"Daaaaaad," she said suspiciously. "You're up to something!"

He scratched the back of his head nervously and flashed a smile.

"Okay, you got me. Come on out to the dining room. I wanna show you that surprise."

He grabbed her hand and led her down the hallway leading to the dining room.

"Close your eyes," he insisted.

He stepped behind her and gently guided her down the hallway. Josie tried to sneak a peek through a crack in her eyelid.

"No peeking, cheater!" He cupped his hands over her eyes and nudged her into the room.

"Now, go ahead," he added. "Open 'em."

Josie's eyes popped open.

"No, you didn't."

"I did," he said proudly. "Happy fifteenth!"

Josie darted across the room to a polished black upright piano set against the far wall. She sat down on the cushioned seat and began tinkling the keys.

"Are you sure you can afford this?" Josie asked.

"Like I said, Josie, I've got some projects lined up."

She tapped the keys like a kid on Christmas morning, the burn of her BFF earlier in the day suddenly not feeling so painful. "My birthday isn't for another ten days!"

"I wanted it to be a surprise," he explained.

"Well, it worked. This piano is amazeballs!"

11

Peter's flight from Bakersfield to Oakland International was two-hundred fifty miles—or a little less than an hour up the central valley and over to the foggy city by the bay.

But, for Peter, having to sit in the same private jet cabin as Sandy made it seem like ten hours. Normally they would be sitting side by side, laptops out, watching a movie or chatting or playing Words with Friends to pass the time. Now he was playing the avoid-eye-contact-at-all-costs game. It was Awkward. Make that AWKWARD.

He wasn't sure whether breaking up with her midtour was the right decision, or if it was the wrong decision at an especially wrong time. When the jet came to a stop in front of the private aviation building and the pilot opened the door, Peter grabbed his travel duffel bag and stepped out into the foggy late afternoon air. He waved to a few dozen fans, who screamed with glee on the other side of a chain-link security fence as he walked down the steps.

Sandy came up to him as he walked across the tarmac to an awaiting car.

They hadn't exchanged a single word on the plane, but Peter knew he couldn't spend the next two months avoiding her like this. They would eventually have to talk.

Peter stopped and faced her as Bobby, Abby, Big Jim, and the rest of the touring crew pulled the baggage from the plane and the entourage filed out of the tricked-out 737 with @PETERMAXXNOW painted on the sides in red and black block letters.

"I'm sorry about last night." Sandy flashed her blue puppy eyes. "I was probably a little harsh."

"I'm sorry too," he immediately melted. "Maybe I shouldn't have said what I did."

"That's the thing," she interrupted, grabbing his hand. "You were right. I think we might be better off as friends. It's just so intense, with the tour, and all the media attention, all the crazy girls always fighting for your attention."

"It's not about other girls," he quickly added. "It's about me, and what I want."

"You're right. I didn't mean it that way. I mean, your fans are my fans. I appreciate them. I was totally wrong last night."

Peter felt relieved. But, more than that, he was shocked. He couldn't believe Sandy was taking being, well, dumped so calmly. "Sandy, you know we'll always be friends." He gave her a hug.

"I know." She pressed her cheek against his.

The squealing fans got louder when they saw Peter and Sandy embrace as Big Jim eyeballed the crowd for any potential fence hoppers.

Sandy released Peter and turned her back to the crowd. She lowered her voice. "The only thing I'm worried about, actually, is the fans. Look at them over there. They love all this Pandy stuff. They're already nuts about our duet coming out in the fall, and if the media found out we weren't dating—and like right in the middle of the tour—it could be a total PR nightmare. For everyone."

He glanced over at a heavyset girl with frizzy black hair decked out in a Peter Maxx concert T-shirt about two sizes too small for her who was poking her camera through a hole in the fence. She was crying. Happy tears. Peter blew her a kiss and she nearly fell over like one of those just-healed churchgoers at the hands of a hyper televangelist.

As much as Peter wanted to make a clean break, he knew Sandy was right. To go public would just create a whole new set of headaches for him: tabloid rumors, the label execs' oldster blood vessels would stroke out, Abby would be fielding calls every day from reporters about who he was or wasn't linked to, and, not that he cared so much, but all those silly gay rumors that hounded him before he began dating Sandy would annoy the heck out of him once again. Plus, it wasn't like he had any other special girl in his life already. In fact, he was looking forward to being alone for a while.

Over and beyond Sandy's left shoulder, Peter could see a couple of paparazzi guys standing on apple boxes, focusing on them with their long-lens cameras just over the fence line. One of the shooters was a stocky guy with dark skin and the other was a white guy in his twenties who always wore a Dodgers cap backward. The two seemed to be everywhere he went.

Always in place to get their shots, taken from different angles from the other, which would immediately download onto their laptops and send to their photo agencies, who would then distribute them instantly to media around the world for purchase. These "exclusive" paparazzi shots (and, lately, one of them was shooting video from a hand-held camera while the other shot still images) often would be blasted all over blogs within a half hour after they were shot.

It was impressive, but scary. No matter how many times Peter asked Abby how the paparazzi knew where and when and with whom he would be showing up so far ahead of time, she never could come up with an answer. The best she could muster was that they were tipped off by "sources." Peter's dad believed the paparazzi, and the reality that people who worked around a celebrity possibly tipped them off, was all just part of the price of fame and that Peter needed to just accept it.

As the paparazzi guys snapped away and the fans kept yelling, Peter gave Sandy another hug. "Maybe I'll see you and everyone later for dinner back at the hotel. Dad set up a group meal in Chinatown."

Sandy pecked him on the cheek and joined the four other G Girls who were impatiently waiting for her in an Escalade. Halfway to the car, Sandy turned around and hopped back to Peter. "I just want to make sure of one thing, but please don't take this the wrong way. I wanna know if this is about you and me, or about your mom. I would hate to see you so haunted by the past for the rest of your life."

"None of the above, Sands. It's about me."

As the crew loaded his baggage into an SUV, Peter walked over to the fence, shaking hands and saying hi to the fans. "How's Sandy?" the curly-haired girl asked.

"She's great. Real great."

"Oh, yeah?" the video-razzi guy asked as he peered down from above. "When's the wedding?"

"Good one," Peter said with a nod, signing a flurry of autographs.

"I want a hug like that girl!" another fan yelled.

Peter looked up from the magazine cover he was signing. "What girl?" he asked the fan.

"You know, the high school girl in Bakersfield you hugged."

"Oh," Peter said, adding, "Well, yeah, I'd hug ya if it weren't for this silly fence!"

Big Jim delivered the bad news to the fans that it was time for them to head out and hustled Peter to the car, jumping into the backseat with him and Bobby.

"How'd that fan know I hugged that girl in Bakersfield?" Peter asked Big Jim, who shrugged his beefy shoulders.

"'Cuz they know everything, Petey," Bobby chimed in as they cruised up onto the majestic Bay Bridge. "That's why I always say if you're gonna hug a fan, do it with one arm. One and done. If you do it with two, you stir too much trouble. Just my advice. Take it or leave it."

"Speaking of Bakersfield," Bobby added, "Before Abby

went back to L.A., she wanted me to remind you to Tweeter about the promotion at the school today. Hot Hollywood asked for it."

"You mean 'Tweet,' Dad," Peter corrected.

"Huh?"

"You told me to 'Tweeter.'"

"Oh, yeah, right," he guffawed. "Tweeter, Twitter. You know what I mean."

Peter had been looking forward to the Oakland tour stop. He had been to the San Francisco Bay Area a couple of times before, but never for a big show like this. He loved the enormous steel bridges, the dramatic views of the water, the moody fog, and the amazing hole-in-the-wall Chinese restaurants. Even though the concert was the next night in Oakland, he'd made sure his dad booked them in the historic Fairmont hotel atop Nob Hill in downtown San Francisco so they could enjoy a night in the city. Since they usually stayed at whatever hotel was closest to the venue, this was a treat for everyone on the tour.

As Peter made his way to the hotel, a road crew was inside Oakland Arena setting up the stage for the next day's show while a second crew was already up in Seattle assembling the stage for his show there. They saved money by having two stage crews working at the same time, avoiding down days in which everyone on the payroll—from the sound engineers to dancers to musicians to security—was being paid to wait for the roadies to construct the set.

By the time Peter plopped onto the bed in his suite on the twenty-third floor it was six o'clock in the evening. He sat up against the elaborately designed backboard and flipped open his laptop to check some e-mail, get on Twitter, check some blogs, and cyber-stalk his buddies. His three best friends—Denny, Roger, and Will—still lived back in Nashville. None of them were in the entertainment business, and with him living in L.A. and being on the road so much, it was easiest to find out what "the good ol' boys" were up to by flicking on Facebook.

Denny would post random pictures of himself in various states of weirdness. Roger, ever the ladies' man, changed his relationship status on a daily basis, his girlfriend changing from one day to the next from petite brunettes to tall blondes. And then back again. Will would post links to the most random videos he could find on YouTube, like the one of the baby telling his landlord to go to hell. During the most intense travel and work days, sometimes his friends' comic relief provided Peter's only laughter of the day.

After stalking his buddies for a few minutes (yes, Roger was suddenly now "in a relationship" with yet another blonde named Britney), he logged onto his Twitter account. Peter had built a loyal following because he actually posted messages himself and didn't use it as a billboard to endorse products. He didn't want his fans to feel like they were constantly being sold something. He wanted at least one forum where he could simply connect.

The purity of Peter's online pursuit had won him over eight million very loyal followers. If there was any bad news it was that he could easily get thousands of messages sent to him every day, making it virtually impossible—no, make that definitely impossible—to read them all. Instead, he would try to scan as many as he could to get an idea of what his fans were obsessing about at any given moment.

On this night, over a thousand fans had re-Tweeted a pic of Peter hugging a ponytailed girl at the Lawndale High event, and several fansites had posted the pic with racy headlines such as "Peter Hugs It Out with Hottie" and "Bakersfield of Dreams." In the fan pic, Peter could see his face, but only the back of the girl. Something about his own face caught his attention. It wasn't the "Peter Perfect" face he usually wore at most fan events, the cool-guy stiff face with the serious eyes that he was told a gazillion times made him look like Ben Stiller striking a *Zoolander*-esque "blue steel" pose. No, he had a wide, almost goofy smile and his eyes were tightly closed.

To Peter, it was the face of happy. He cracked a smile just looking at it. He had probably met over a hundred kids that day, shook hands, posed for pics, signed autographs. He had gone through the machinations of a promo appearance just as he had so many hundreds of times before. More often than not, Peter would meet and greet with so many fans he couldn't remember any single one. But Peter didn't have a problem remembering the brown-eyed girl who had written that contest song, who had worn that "Music Is My Boyfriend" shirt, the girl some twelve hours after the fact he was seeing in the picture. She on her tippy toes as he two-arm hugged her inside the classroom. There was a connection. And now his hyperobservant fans had noticed.

Peter had assumed that when he became a global pop superstar and people everywhere knew his name and face and he had become famous beyond even his dad's wildest dreams that he'd become the happiest person on the planet. Turned out, he was wrong. Turned out, he wanted to change it.

Maybe the emptiness came from spending so much time hanging around adults who in any other reality would have no business hanging around people so much younger than him. Maybe it was from dropping out of high school and getting tutored so he could work—and avoid being hassled by fans and media. He didn't know for sure.

What he did know was that in the last two years he had gone from being a kid on a TV show who could go to the movies and not be noticed, to being a household name and face who long ago stopped trying to do the normal things a teenager does because, well, it had started to become too dangerous: the mobs and the cops being called for crowd control. The hysterical fans couldn't let him just enjoy a frozen yogurt at the Hermosa Beach pier, so he had started to wear a wig and giant glasses and, suddenly, he felt like a freak, like a latter-day Michael Jackson—only not so weird. At least not yet.

Peter Maxx didn't want to become another child-star stat, another unsympathetic "victim" paying the so-called "price of fame." He didn't want his sanity to be a lamb sacrificed to the fame gods.

He instead wanted to follow a different path. He wanted to know what it was like to go to a high school dance, what it was like to date a girl who wasn't famous, what it felt like to be surrounded by kids his own age, what it felt like to make a love connection with a real girl—not Girl Group Barbie. Someone *normal*—a girl who had a life entirely outside of what his dad liked to call "Hollyweird."

His hotel room's panoramic view beckoning, Peter got off his bed and walked to the floor-to-ceiling glass window that looked out on the Golden Gate Bridge. In the distance, even through the thick window, he could hear a foghorn blowing as the thick mist rolled in from the chilly Pacific waters. Other high-rise hotels and apartment buildings sprouted up below his window high atop Nob Hill. An antique brass telescope sat positioned on a tripod in front of the window.

Peter turned off the lamp in his suite. His heart began racing.

Cocking shut his left eye and placing his widened right eye in front of the viewfinder, he pointed the telescope in the direction of an apartment directly across the street from his hotel. It was Friday night. Real people went out on Friday nights, right?

He focused into a room on the corner of the twenty-second floor. He saw a couple of kids sitting on a couch watching TV. Peter panned over to the neighboring window into a bedroom and saw a woman—their mom?—standing in front of a vanity mirror putting on makeup. She was dressed up in an elegant sleeveless black dress and in what appeared to be heels.

He could now see that the two kids were teenagers. A boy and girl. They were eating popcorn. Might they even be watching *For Pete's Sake?* A man walked in from another room in a fancy suit and tie and started talking to them. He leaned down and kissed both kids on the forehead and said a few more words before the woman walked in and did the same. As Peter huddled behind the telescope watching, saying to himself, *So normal. So normal. So normal.*

Peter slid the telescope back from the window. For all he knew, paparazzi could be staked out across his hotel shooting him spying on the people. He could just imagine the tabloid headline: "Peter Pervert!" He snapped shut the heavy curtains and then, fumbling in the dark, turned the lamp back on.

Then he picked up his laptop and knelt down on the floor and, using the bed as a desk, began typing. At the advice of his father and Abby, Peter had never before followed a fangirl on Twitter; moreover, he had never direct-messaged a fan with a private message. Until now.

12

Josie got a kick out of watching her dad barbecue, mostly because he wasn't a very good cook. He had a tendency to burn hot dogs to a crisp by putting them on too early ahead of the burgers and had an epic knack for undercooking burgers so much you could almost hear them moo on the bun.

Yet the enthusiasm Kyle Brant brought to the backyard grill defied his profound lack of expertise. He wore an apron on which was printed in red letters: KISS THE COOK. By the grill, he kept a cutlery set that included a silver spatula, a two-prong fork, an eight-inch knife, and a scraper. By the looks of the blackened rack, the scraper hadn't been used for a while. If, in fact, ever.

Josie could smell the charred remains burning in the backyard as she sat in the dining room at her upright piano, humming along to some simple chord progressions. She had owned the same Casio keyboard for the last five years, but never a piano. The only time she ever got to play a real piano was at Ashley's house, where her family kept a shiny baby grand in their living room that was touched more by their housekeeper's feather duster than someone's fingers. Josie noticed how the keys were much heavier than those on her keyboard; no one ever taught her how to work the pedals to damper and amplify the sounds, but whenever she sat down on the bench it made her feel like a real songwriter.

The piano in her dad's house was not quite as fancy as Ashley's baby grand. It was a black Yamaha, as good as new, though her dad said he got a "good deal" off a used instrument website. He wouldn't say how much he spent, but Josie knew it was over a thousand bucks. If his goal was to make her want to come to his house more often now that the summer vacation was near, it was working. She could picture spending afternoons playing and writing songs, perhaps even finally learning some of those '90s hits that Christopher exposed her to. She couldn't wait to show Christopher.

"Now you can be the next Katy Perry," her dad announced through the wall as he listened from the kitchen prepping his meats.

"Maybe," Josie shouted back. "If I could actually sing!"

"Well, you're a talented hummer. You could be the first famous hummer to be on *American Idol.*"

Josie kept tapping the keys. "I'll just stick with writing. The rejection is less harsh on the ego."

"Well, then you can use it to write songs. Maybe you'll write some real masterpieces in this shack now." Holding the platter, he poked his head through the doorway. "Two veggie burgers, right?"

"Just one."

"Let's go with two just in case."

"Fine. But I probably will only have one."

"Sarah will eat the other one," he said, walking out and heading for the back door.

Sarah? Oh, no. Hopefully not another bimbo girlfriend he met at the bar. Hopefully not another girl in her twenties who had a crush on him when he played hockey when they were still in high school. Sarah. That name just sounded to her like the wrong kind of woman for her dad. Josie didn't want him to be alone the rest of his life, but since she had seen so many random chicks come and go, she had grown understandably cynical about his various romances. Especially one named "Sarah."

The only girlfriend she had ever really liked was Jessie, who worked in the dispatch department of his oil company and absolutely adored her dad. She had kind, dark eyes, naturally wavy hair like from a shampoo ad, and, most important, was respectful toward Josie, even once telling her, "You don't have to like me or even want me around. I get it. I just want you to know my heart is pure, and you can tell me anything."

Jessie was pretty, but not so attractive that she had gotten used to being given things in life because of her looks. Her dad had a tendency to fall for those kind of girls—the lipstick and eye shadowed-out blondes with beauty queen bodies and intellects as shallow as a kiddie pool. #JustSayNoToBimbos.

As for this "Sarah" lady, Josie would reserve judgment until she could kick her tires and give her a test drive. All her dad asked when it came to new girlfriends was that Josie try not to compare them to her mom. But even though her mom had been getting on her nerves lately, when it came down to it, Josie respected her mom for always being there for her. The last thing Josie wanted was for some lady to come along that made her mother feel bad about herself, made her wonder whether she wasn't cute enough, or young enough. Josie didn't want to endure overhearing another conversation her mom was having with a girlfriend debating if she should get Botox or not. #OldLadyProblems.

Josie's ideal girlfriend for her dad: smart, friendly, employed, slightly above-average looking, but not spectacular. This was Jessie. The only problem was that since she was a hard-core Christian and Josie's dad informed her he didn't "do the church thing," the relationship ended faster than a hockey game that goes into a sudden death shootout.

Josie wondered how either her mom or dad could believe in true love ever again, especially when they went from being the most adorable and in love couple in town to being two parents arguing all the time. Certainly, it made Josie question it, and she herself had never even been in love.

> *They say every glove has a hand that fits*
> *They say there's someone for everyone*
> *I say but how can I believe in such a need*
> *When I see all hearts bleed*

As Josie found a C sharp chord that matched the lyrics, she heard a car door slam.

She got up from her piano, and through the front door

screen she saw Connor walking up in his baseball uniform. Sure, he could be a little pest, but on this hot summer evening she had to give him props for being a little cutie in his uniform.

"How was practice, superstar?" she asked as he walked inside.

"Good, but I'm hungry," he grumbled.

Josie watched him glumly walk by without looking at her. She followed him into the bedroom. "Yeah, yeah, yeah," he said, dropping his backpack on the bed. "I know why you're so happy. I heard you met Peter Maxx. Everyone was talking about it at school. Congrats. You finally lost your virginity."

"Don't be a scuz." She knocked him playfully in the arm. "But, I'm not gonna lie, it was cool. But it's not the *only* reason I'm smiling."

"Okay, I hope it involves food because I am starving."

"No food. But Dad got me a piano. It's so cool. Check it out."

"I'm soooo happy for you," Connor said, popping his eyeballs. "Even happier if he threw down some cashola for my new Xbox."

"Well, he's been in a giving mood today, so I wouldn't count it out."

Josie's phone buzzed atop the nightstand between their two beds. It buzzed again. Then again. It began buzzing so much it almost fell off the table.

Josie picked it up and saw that she had almost a hundred text messages and Facebook alerts. And they weren't just stalking texts from Ashley, and they weren't messages from Christopher offering a shoulder to cry on, though there were a couple of those too. Most were about the hug. Unbeknownst to Josie, an hour ago a Lawndale student posted it on her Twitter and ever since it had been ricocheting around the Web.

Whoa. Check out pics on OMC. Holy whaaa!

wtf! He hugged you. How rad!

I hear wedding bells

"Oh my God. Oh my God. Oh my God. Oh my God." Josie couldn't believe what she was seeing. The hug was special, for sure. But now her entire school, not to mention the entire Peter fandom, had seen their affectionate embrace.

Josie collapsed butt-first onto her bed and tapped her phone keys like her life depended on it. She clicked on all the random links to blogs that were chattering about the pic. Several fansites were calling Josie a "mystery girl" because you couldn't see her face in the photo. Just the backside of her—and Peter's unusually relaxed face.

"Why are you freaking out?" Connor asked.

"Connor." She gulped. "I think I'm sort of famous." She showed him the hugging pic on her phone. "Look."

Connor strained his eyes to bring the image into focus. "Wow," he said. "Too bad you didn't wash your hair this morning."

Connor studied the photo more closely. "All right. Yeah. He probably likes you."

"How can you tell?" she asked eagerly.

"It's obvious."

"Like how?"

"Like I have never seen that guy hug a fan like that."

Josie didn't know whether her brother was jerking her chain or if he was serious. "Doesn't matter either way. I'll probably never see him again."

"So we won't be moving into a mansion and living like rock stars," Connor quipped, stepping into the bathroom. "Because I'm all about that."

Josie ran through the kitchen out to the backyard, where her father was carefully placing a slice of processed yellow cheese onto a sizzling hamburger.

"Dad, this is unbelievable! Check this out!"

He put the spatula down and took hold of her phone, blinking his eyes several times. She couldn't tell if her dad was clearing the smoke from his eyes or if he couldn't believe his little girl was something of a celebrity.

"I take it this is that Peter kid, eh?"

"Yeah."

"I've seen him on TV. You like him, eh?"

"Obviously."

He messed up her hair with a twist of his palm, handed the phone back to her, and turned his attention back to the barbecue.

"Be careful." He pressed the juice out of a patty. "The hottest things in life also can burn you the most."

Cheese melted down the sides and into the charcoal, spitting puffs of black smoke into the air. The brownish-orange sun began its slow drop toward the western horizon off the side yard fence, just beyond the Frito-Lay plant.

Like clockwork for around early summer, a cool breeze blew in from the west just after seven, sweeping the hot, sticky air out. Fresh air—just what Josie's life needed. Finally, with meeting Peter Maxx, with getting her own piano, with being so at peace with her life for the first time in a long time, she felt like she was getting it.

Her dad served up the burgers on paper plates and squirted ketchup all over them. Connor inhaled two juicy cheeseburgers and a stack of chips inside while watching TV. Josie, meanwhile, sat beside her dad on the back porch step and nibbled her charred veggie burger.

Her phone kept vibrating in her front pocket. "Hey, honey, at least turn it off while we eat," her dad requested. "I'm sure your pop star will still be there when you turn it back on." She complied and put it down on the wooden porch floor.

As Josie's dad ate, he kept standing up and looking out over the back fence, as if looking for someone. "You know, Josie, if you're paying attention, working in the oil fields teaches you a lot about life." He sat down. "Watching those oil pumps bobbing makes you realize life is up and down just like that. But as long as you keep pumping, you eventually will fill up the barrel."

Josie wanted to say, "Yeah, but oil drilling is also bad for the environment." Not wanting to kill his buzz, she instead changed the subject.

"Dad," she said, snapping him back to attention. "Do you ever miss Mom?"

"I miss the good days, yeah. But I don't miss the bad days." He gnawed a little more on his cheeseburger. "But I do miss all of us being together as a family. Those were some great days."

"I don't understand how everything could go from being so good to being so bad. Kind of makes me feel like love is a feeling you can't trust. I mean, did you just wake up one day and things were bad?"

"No, it happened over time. We stopped talking, stopped caring about each other, stopped being curious about each other. Maybe we just ran out of gas. I don't know." He paused. "My drinking didn't help. I know that."

Josie tilted her head. "I still don't get it. Makes you think there's no hope for true love."

He looked out at the backyard. "If I had all the answers, Josie, maybe I would have my own talk show. Like Dr. Phil."

"Yeah, Dr. Kyle. The doctor of dysfunction."

"Hey, as long as I don't have to get fat and bald, I'm in. We could move to Hollywood and live the high life."

Josie liked that her dad was a dreamer, and that he still had the spirit of a kid who thought that life could be a fairy tale, that he could someday win the lottery, move to Hollywood, and live happily ever after.

Puffy white bunnies and princess tales
Maidens and moons and that cute little mouse,
    goodnight to all
Scraping whiskers on my cheek
All grown now, no more mouse
Backyard talks on the porch of the house
I still love you

"How about we hear some piano?" her dad said as they finished up their dinner.

"Sounds good to me." Josie finished her veggie burger and stacked her dad's empty plate onto hers. After dumping them in the garbage can next to the house, Josie used the moment to sneak a peek at her phone.

It vibrated back to life in her hand, illuminating her face in the twilight. A Twitter direct message alert popped up. She opened it.

@PeterMaxxNow hi @MusicLuvr. Write any good songs lately?

13

Immediately after he pressed Send, Peter feared the worst-case fangirl scenarios that his publicist and Bobby were always warning him about.

What if "@MusicLuvr" was a stalker? What if she was the kind of girl to tell the world that a famous guy just messaged her? What if she had a protective psycho father who read all her messages and would freak out on him? He didn't even know how old she was. Fourteen? Fifteen? Maybe she was only thirteen and looked old for her age. If Peter weren't so honest, he could always deny he sent the message, do what other celebrities do and have Abby put out a statement claiming he was hacked or something. But Peter never wanted to lie to his fans.

Breathe.

Realizing he was running late for dinner, Peter slipped on his high-tops and a Windbreaker and hustled down to the lobby to meet up with his entourage: Bobby; Abby; the five G Girls; his tour manager, Scout; Denny the sound guy; Phil the lighting guy; and Big Jim.

"We were just about to leave without you!" Bobby exclaimed when Peter appeared at the valet stand. "Mister Woo's Kitchen awaits. . . . Where's your phone?"

"In my room, duh."

"Thatta boy."

Bobby had a rule for group dinners: they were always "unplugged" get-togethers. Bobby had a theory that people nowadays didn't talk and get to know each other enough. They were constantly distracted by their phones, texting other people instead of actually interacting with those around them. "When I was young we would sit on the porch and jabber all night," he said. As a result, his Chinese-food feast wasn't just about eating delicious food, but also about everyone connecting.

Bobby had arranged for the entire table of twelve to ride a vintage red cable car down California Street into Chinatown. When the rickety car creaked to a stop in front of the hotel and the conductor rang the bell, the entourage excitedly hopped aboard. The same two paparazzi guys from the Oakland Airport earlier in the day snapped away from across the street. Peter's freshly minted ex-girlfriend plopped beside him on the riding bench. Sandy leaned in and whispered, "Well, we might as well make it look good in public."

"Good idea," Peter agreed.

"Have you told anyone we broke up? 'Cuz I haven't."

"Just Big Jim. And only because he was standing there the whole time and heard it anyway."

"Well, you can fire his ass if he told anyone. Right?"

"Technically yes. But I'd never have to do that. Jimbo's solid."

"I didn't mean it that way," Sandy apologized.

"I know," Peter said. Before, he would have been annoyed by her trash-talking Jim, would have taken it personally. Now that they had broken up, he just felt sad for her.

Peter's body was sitting in the cable car, his eyes watching the tourists on the sidewalks, his mouth moving as he talked to Sandy, but his mind was still back on what he had just done in his hotel room. It represented more to him than just an online flirtation. He felt like he had started a new chapter and, for the first time in a while, he was excited to explore something new with somebody new. Of course, he would never tell Sandy this, so he just chitchatted her with an emotional distance he might have with a stranger on a bus.

"How do you feel?" he asked.

"Great," Sandy answered. "I'm already getting used to this friends thing. Seriously."

"Good." Peter nodded and smiled, patting her on the thigh in that unaffectionate, friend-to-friend way. "Glad we're on the same page. Now let's eat."

Dumplings. Green tea. Wonton soup. Sweet-and-sour chicken. Chow mein. Szechuan chicken. Moo Shu pork. The table was covered in steaming plates and bowls, a feast fit for a king, or at least a pop star. Other diners couldn't help but notice the famous singer sitting at the large table in the back of the crowded restaurant. Peter was used to the attention. He had learned to block it out. He imagined that's what gorillas did at the zoo. They just came to accept that some random stranger was always looking at them, even as they ate, slept and scratched their privates. Being a celebrity wasn't too different than being a zoo creature, but the pay was better—as was the food.

"Excuse me, mister. You the famous singer?" the tuxedoed server asked Peter.

"Yes."

"My niece loves you. Take picture?"

Abby sprinted over to Peter's chair. "I'm sorry, sir," she said abruptly. "We'd rather Peter be left alone while he eats. Thank you."

"So sorry. So sorry." The waiter nodded and shuffled backward.

Peter felt bad for the guy.

"It's cool, Abby," he said. "The guy just wants a picture for his niece. It's okay."

Abby bent over Peter's ear. "Look around you. There are fifty people in this place who want to do the same thing. If you do it for one, then you'll have to do it for everyone, and you won't be able to get out of here alive, let alone eat your dinner."

By now, the ashamed waiter had disappeared back into the kitchen. What Abby said made sense, but it also didn't seem right.

The rest of the dinner party was eating and laughing at Bobby's clumsy use of chopsticks. They didn't notice. But Big Jim did. From across the table, he caught Peter's attention with a lift of his chin and pointed to the kitchen with his right thumb over his shoulder and they both got up and walked away from the table. The two met up in front of the swinging doors separating the kitchen from the dining room, and Big Jim led Peter back into the pungent kitchen and approached the waiter, who was scooping soup into bowls. The waiter winced at the sight of the security guard towering over him.

"Sir, you still want that picture?" Big Jim said.

"Uh, I did, sir, yes." The waiter excitedly handed Jim the camera.

Peter sidled beside the friendly man and rested his left arm around the waiter's shoulders, and Jim snapped away.

"Thank you, Thank you so very much." The man glowed.

"No worries," Peter told him as he patted him on the back. "What's your niece's name?"

"Anna," he said. "She's fourteen. She real big fan. Big fan."

"Well, tell her I said 'hi' for me."

As Peter made his way back to his table and finished his Asian feast, his mind still came back not to the millions of fans, but back to one. That girl in Bakersfield. If he had his phone, he would have been obsessively checking to see if she replied.

Instead, Peter sat in his chair sucking down noodles and laughing at the jokes his dad told about everyone at their own expense. Five years ago, Bobby would have been downing beers as he held court, and probably would have been a lot louder and a lot more obnoxious. But when Peter signed his record deal, Bobby vowed he'd go dry—and he did. "Life gives you second chances," he told his son the day he dumped his last case of beer down the kitchen drain. "Never third chances."

Peter stared at the saucy noodles on his plate. He studied how some stuck together, intertwined around another, while others just lay alone, unable to connect to others. He didn't want to be a lone noodle.

As he pondered his plate wisdom, his mind went back to that crowded classroom in Bakersfield, back to eye-connecting with a girl who emanated innocence and purity and integrity. A girl whom he was feeling stuck on. The gawky girl with the sweet brown eyes and a ponytail that dropped perfectly between her shoulder blades. The girl whose T-shirt declared that music was her boyfriend. She wasn't Hollywood beautiful, but she was normal beautiful. Looking at pictures of his mom, Peter often noticed she had a similar kind of beauty. The kind that didn't need a three-hundred-dollar haircut and team of beauty handlers to create.

It was becoming clear to Peter that he had a crush—on a fangirl.

Meanwhile, on the opposite side of the table Sandy and her other G Girls gossiped about God-knows-what as they pretended to eat baby-size pieces of food. From the outside looking in, the scene might have looked like good food, friends, even family. But Peter couldn't enjoy the moment, because he couldn't get that girl out of his mind. He wanted her there with him.

The waiter returned to the table with the check, along with a plate stacked with plastic-wrapped fortune cookies. Peter had a tradition whenever he went to a Chinese restaurant: he would pass the plate of cookies around and make each person pick one, with him going last. It didn't matter what others picked or that he may have missed out on one if he picked earlier. The breathing-based meditation therapy he had been doing recently had taught him that the most important thing in life was to be present. God takes care of everything else. Indeed, he believed in fate, even when it came to reading cheesy fortune cookies.

Peter got up and walked around the circular table, and each of the diners chose a treat. The last to select was Sandy and, as it turned out, she took the last cookie. "Looks like you have no fortune." Sandy giggled. Her expression turned bitter. So did her tone. "How ironic," she said smugly.

The waiter stepped to the table and handed Peter a cookie. "Where I'm from," he said, "last is lucky." Peter nodded in agreement.

"Okay," Peter announced to the group. "Clockwise. You go first, Jimmy."

Big Jim split open his cookie with his giant hands as if opening a tiny book and pulled a slip of paper from the crumbled mess. "Like a closed mouth gathers no food, a closed mind gathers no wisdom." The table exploded in laughter. "Amen!" he said, dropping the treat in his mouth.

As they went around the table there were the typical ones

("Happiness is a state of mind" for Bobby) and the generic ("You will live a long and happy life" for Abby). Then it came to Sandy. She cracked open hers, careful not to chip her bright-red fingernail polish. "Beauty is more than skin deep," she read aloud to the group.

Everyone at the table had heard her, but no one offered up a reaction. "How ironic," Peter quipped. The table nervously laughed—all but for Sandy.

"Ha-ha," she sneered.

Peter bit off an end of the cookie, slowly plucked out the thin strip of paper, and cleared his throat with dramatic flair. He flashed a smile. "Trust your heart."

"Cheers to that!" Bobby announced as he lifted his glass of water.

Peter folded the message and slid it into his jeans pocket.

Back at the hotel shortly before midnight, Peter high-fived and bro-hugged his crew goodnight before they went up the elevator to their rooms. Everyone, that is, but Sandy. She was MIA.

"Where's Sandy?" Peter asked Molly, the other petite blond G Girl.

"She already went upstairs. She said something about some stuff she had to do."

So did Peter. Once inside his hotel room, Peter shot a bee-line straight for his phone. He powered it on, but the screen stayed black. Oh, crap. He forgot to charge the battery. He grabbed his laptop off the bed, plopped down on the sitting-area couch, and flipped open his laptop. He was too tired to look at all his @replies. Tonight, he only cared about reading one fan: @MusicLuvr. But there, at the top where the newest messages were displayed, was nothing. Not a single reply.

A lonely noodle, indeed.

14

Josie remembered reading the Tweet from Peter and her heart skipping a beat. Gasping for air. Blinking to make sure she was reading what her eyes told her she was reading, that it was real. That she was someone who mattered enough for him to write to her.

She felt special—with a future as bright as the slanting colors of orange angling across the flat farmland. But then the next events played in her mind like a movie that she had memorized line by line, shot by shot, a movie in which she was just another character in the unfolding drama, someone caught up in a moment of which she had no control.

The sound of the crickets in the fields was gradually drowned out by the *whoosh* of a low-flying helicopter hovering over the house.

Connor ran out to Josie and stared skyward while her father dropped the spatula and ran inside.

An army of uniformed men in visor helmets and bullet-proof vests charged through the backyard fence door pointing guns at them.

"Down. Get down!" they told them.

And so they did.

"No! 'Face down,' we said. On your bellies!"

And so they did.

"Drop everything!" Josie dropped her phone to the ground next to her brother who lay frozen on the cut grass like a corpse. "Do what we say and everything will be fine. Do not move until we tell you."

"It's okay, it's okay, it's okay. Don't worry, Connor. It's okay, it's okay, it's okay."

"Suspect ran inside. Get him!"

"Is he armed?"

"Don't know, Chief."

"Keep your weapons drawn, boys."

"Mr. Brant, come out now and no one will get hurt!" The guy repeated himself, and his body armor jostled as he ran toward the doorstep. "You have ten seconds to walk out that door before we use force. We have a search warrant, Mr. Brant."

"Get the kids out of here," the guy in charge yelled to the others.

A man grabbed her arms back like chicken wing bones. "Get up. Move it!"

"Connor. Where's Connor?"

"Don't worry. He's safe."

Some had holsters on their belts, walkie-talkies strapped to them like something out of *G.I. Joe*. Others had holsters tied around their thighs, too. Some had both and wore combat boots thumping as they walked—like Stormtroopers. Only these commandos were real.

Josie felt a forceful push down onto the ground next to the oak tree in the front yard—on her butt. The man turned around. On the back of his jacket in bright yellow letters was the name DEA. What the heck was that?

The helicopter was still circling.

"Where's my phone?"

"Don't worry about that, honey. That's the least of your problems."

"What's going on? Why are you doing this to us?"

"Ask your dad, honey. He knows what's going on."

She was shaky. Her lungs tightened. A panic attack had begun. If only her lungs weren't so tight, she would suck in the night air. But she couldn't.

She heard yelling in the backyard. "Suspect in custody," the voice crackled on the walkie-talkies.

They found Josie's dad inside the house. He was sitting on the piano bench. "Hands up! Don't touch the piano. I said 'HANDS UP,' sir!"

"You're under arrest. You have the right to remain silent."

"He armed? No. Okay, take him downtown."

"The kids? Call next of kin."

Connor was brought to the tree by two armed men who plopped him down next to her. She gripped his hand. Tightly. For dear life.

"I don't understand, Josie. I don't understand. Are we in trouble, Josie?"

"I don't think so."

15

As much as Peter could dish out the silent treatment, he did-
n't take it very well when the tables were turned on
him—especially when he really wanted to hear back from
someone, especially when it was a girl he liked.

Maybe Josie was busy? Or, possibly, she didn't think it was
really him Tweeting her. It was pretty random for him to reach
out to a fan directly, after all. Or maybe she didn't have a cell
phone or access to a computer? No, everyone had a phone and
a computer. Maybe he wrote down the wrong username?

He Googled her: "Josie Bakersfield Twitter."

Nothing but hundreds of random results.

He typed in "MusicLuvr."

At the top of the results was a link to her profile:

@MusicLuvr bakersfield,ca
Changing the world one song at a time

The Twitter profile pic looked exactly like her. And the
messages in her profile all but confirmed it. Most were about
music or, more importantly, sweet, supportive messages to him.
How did I not ever read these? Oh yeah. I get thousands a day. Her last
Tweet was from Peter's Bakersfield show, a pic of him onstage
along with the message, "Heaven."

Boom, boom, boom! Three forceful knocks on his door. *It better be important*, Peter thought. It was past midnight.

"Open up," barked a deep voice on the other side of his hotel door. "It's the police!"

"Yeah, yeah," Peter said, reaching to open the door. "Nice try."

Standing before Peter in the doorway was Big Jim, fashioning his finger and thumb into the shape of a pistol with his right hand and holding a bottle of water in his left. "Always wanted to be a cop, but my knees are shot." He ambled past Peter. "So now I get the pleasure of babysitting you—you know, feeding and watering you like my Chihuahua puppy."

"Woof-woof," Peter barked.

"I'm just seeing if you need anything before I crash for the night. Was just lookin' at the itinerary. Long day tomorrow. You got the show over in Oakland and then right after we fly down to L.A. And oh . . ." Big Jim handed Peter the jumbo-size bottle of water. "Your pa said you gotta drink this before you go to bed. Something about 'lubricating' your vocal chords."

"Please tell me he did not really use the word 'lubricating.'"

"I swear, he did." Big Jim laughed. "I couldn't make that up."

Jim noticed the opened laptop on the coffee table by the couch. "Speaking of Jesus. You watchin' dirty videos again? 'Cuz God just isn't gonna approve of . . ."

"What do you mean *again*?" Peter scurried over to the table and slamming the laptop closed. Jim erupted in one of his signature belly laughs that sent his rotund stomach heaving up and down like a shaken bowl of jelly.

"Relax. Just jokin' with ya."

"Good one. You really wanna know what I was doing?"

"I don't know." Jim cracked a mischievous smile. "You tell me."

Peter sat on the couch and opened back up his laptop.

"If you really must know, well, I'm stalking a fan."

"What? You're stalking a stalker? Now that's funny."

"Well, I don't know if she's a stalker," Peter corrected. "In fact . . ." Peter refreshed his Twitter for the fifth time in the last minute. "The girl won't even write me back."

"Bummer, huh? But now you know what it's like for the rest of us dudes who live in *reality*. You were a rejection virgin. This is a first for you. You should be proud."

"First time for everything." Peter sighed.

"How's it feel to get thrown the Heisman?"

"Not good."

Jim gently patted Peter between his shoulder blades. "If it makes ya feel any better, I've been turned down more times than the volume on your iPod."

Peter kept surfing. "Just make sure you don't tell Dad. He'll kill me."

Peter knew Bobby might just blow a major fuse, especially because, with gospel-like fervor, he had instructed his son, "The first two rules of dating a fan are . . . Number One: Don't do it. And . . ." This is where Bobby would flash two stiff fingers. "Number Two: Still don't do it."

Peter looked out the window at the apartment building across the street. The curtains were pulled closed in front of the window he had peered into earlier in the night. "Either way," Peter continued. "He'd be real mad."

"Trust me, I know. My job's makin' sure you don't get kidnapped or die. So telling your dad you were stalking a fan, well, that would kinda make me bad at my job now, wouldn't it?"

"Good man," Peter said, with a fist bump.

"So who's the girl?"

"I met her down in Bakersfield this morning."

"Ah, the cute little chick in the hat."

"How'd you know?"

Jim plopped his plump self down on the couch. "Son, I've been around the block. I saw that whole thing goin' down."

"What *thing*? The hug? I hug, basically, every fan. C'mon, dude." Peter knew he was sounding defensive.

"Not the hug, Romeo. I saw what you did to her hair. You flicked her hair."

"And your point?"

"My point is that a guy only plays with a girl's hair when he's really into her. Kid, I watched you bop around with Sandy for like the last year, and I never once saw you do that to her. Not once."

Peter didn't have a comeback for that one.

"Just be careful," Jim added.

"Why?" Peter asked with a smirk.

"First of all—no offense—but you don't even know this girl. Plus, all the Web wing nuts are already up your butt on this one."

"Well, discretion is the better part of valor."

"What?"

"It's Shakespeare. Word!"

"Wow, I guess that tutor really is teaching you somethin', isn't she."

"You know it," Peter said. "Anyway, it means that I just have to be careful to keep it secret and I'll be okay."

"Good luck with that one. And she has to write you back first, remember. As of now, you're just hanging naked out there in your birthday suit."

"True."

Jim added, "Just, do me a favor, make sure she's a fan—and not a Stan."

"Stan" was an old Eminem song about an obsessed fan, but Big Jim coined the word as meaning a wack-job fan, a girl who might kidnap her idol, stuff him in her trunk, and kill him—or maybe even kill herself, because she's so obsessed with him.

Part of Big Jim's job was to always separate fans from Stans.

"Well, you've got the best Stan radar in the business. What's your Stan-o-meter say about this girl?"

"Lemme see her again," Jim said.

Peter flipped up his laptop and opened up her Twitter

page, revealing Josie's smiling face with the dimpled cheeks and warm, walnut-colored eyes. Jim studied the picture and scrolled through her posts.

Then he shook his head, handed the laptop back to Peter, and got up.

"Okay, I've seen enough." He shuffled his hefty body toward the door. "My work is done."

"So what's the verdict?" Peter followed closely behind him. "You just can't walk off and not tell me. So not cool."

Jim turned the handle and opened the door. Before stepping into the hallway, he turned back to Peter and said with a smile, "Don't worry. She's cool."

◄◄ ■ ►►|

"Now breathe in as deeply as you can, and now slowly through your nose . . . and let it out your mouth. . . . Nice, Peter. Now just let it all go."

Peter had never asked, but he guessed his therapist had to be close to seventy years old. She had studied clinical psychology, even gotten a PhD in it, but for the last twenty years had come to believe that traditional "talk" psychotherapy could only go so far, especially when it came to healing deep-seated anxiety and past traumas, experiences that seemed to be burned into patients' brains as if with a branding iron.

Peter had been seeing her for the last six months, and the results for him were nothing short of miraculous. The mere thought of his mom no longer sent him into an emotional tailspin and into darkness. The general sense of anxiety and worry over all the pressures of being a pop star suddenly seemed manageable. With each deep breath, each meditation session, he felt the pain blowing out of him like steam from a tea kettle.

The Oakland concert had gone well. Another sellout. Another arena filled with adoring fans. Now it was Sunday, and he had the day off before leaving Monday for a string of back-to-back nights: Kansas City (Tuesday), Denver (Wednesday), and two shows in Vegas (Friday and Saturday). The meditation sessions left him feeling so energized and refreshed and healed that he made sure to book an hour-long appointment with Judith on his rare day off—and again the following Sunday since he would have two days back in L.A. before picking back up the tour in Seattle.

Judith just sat on a chair a few feet from the table. "What do you feel in your body?" she asked calmly.

Peter took another couple of breaths, followed by equally deep and long exhales. He could feel his legs and arms sinking into the table. He hadn't yet drifted into a meditative state, but he could sense he was getting close.

"I feel still."

"That's good, Peter. Feeling still is peaceful. What else do you feel?"

Peter kept his steady breathing and softly replied, "I feel tingling in my fingers."

"Ooh, that's a good thing. That means you're getting

oxygen to your body. The breathing is working. Focus on your breathing. Do you see any colors, shapes, or images?"

"Yes. I see my mom's face."

"What's she doing?"

"Sleeping."

"But your mom is no longer alive, right, Peter?"

"She isn't."

"So she isn't sleeping."

"No." His bottom lip began to quiver.

"How does that make you feel?" Judith asked.

Peter sucked in a pocket of air and filled his lungs to the stretching point and released. His lip trembled. "I feel sad. Real sad."

"Peter," Judith continued. "If your mom were here, what would you tell her?"

"I miss you. I really miss you."

The tears trapped under his eyelids were now leaking through the sides of his eyes. They rolled down each of his cheeks, collecting in his ears. His arms were too heavy to lift them. He felt their warmth.

"Were you close to your mom?" Judith asked.

"I was closer to her than anyone. And anyone since."

"I could see why you would miss her."

Judith gently placed her hands on his abdomen. "Breathe through it, Peter. It's okay."

Peter took a deep inhale and out came a burst of air and a wailing sound—a sad, crying, choppy rush of air ending with a slight moan. And then came another. Judith continued to rub his stomach as if loosening up the blockage that had been keeping him from totally releasing his emotions. "I miss my best friend. She was my best friend."

An hour after the session began, it ended. He gradually came out of his hypnotic state, opening his eyes and wiggling his toes, focusing his gaze on his surroundings.

"Why are you smiling?" Judith asked.

"Because of a girl." He was now sitting up on the padded table.

"A girl you like, I take it?"

"Yes. I think I'm ready, definitely ready."

"Ready for what?" she asked softly.

"I'm ready to move on with my life, be my own man."

Peter swallowed, then breathed in deeply and out and calmly added, "I'm ready to really love someone."

16

Josie lay on her back staring at her bedroom ceiling. Despite her profound exhaustion, she couldn't fall asleep. Her nerves were so frayed, her mind so busy with a confusing stream of consciousness, that a Sunday afternoon nap was out of the question.

The scene kept playing out in her mind: after the cops had arrested her dad inside the house, they had cuffed him and had walked him out to a van as Connor and Josie had sat beneath the giant oak tree in stunned silence.

"I'm sorry," he had mouthed before the cops had placed him in the van and took him down to the Kern County jail. That's where they had also taken Josie and Connor, though they hadn't placed them in custody. They had done nothing wrong; they were just "victims of circumstance," the cops had explained to Josie and Connor before calling their mom to come get them at headquarters.

Around midnight, Josie's mom had arrived. She had been in L.A. with Thomas, and when she had gotten the voice mail from the police she had immediately sped up the freeway, going over a hundred miles an hour. She had seen Connor and Josie sitting on the floor in the lobby next to the reception desk when she had arrived, and had hugged them both like she would never let go.

Josie had told her mom the police had said they were free to leave, that they were only witnesses and likely would be asked to testify at some point down the road. Now they could just go home.

Officer Rick Sanchez, a short man with a friendly smile whose wife had worked with Josie's mom at the clinic, approached the three of them. "Kimberly, everything is fine. We just wanted to protect the children. We didn't know if there were smugglers in the area, and we needed to lock the place down. We took good care of them."

"Thanks, Ricky. Now can you tell me what the hell is going on?"

He had explained that for the last year or so Kyle had been illegally growing medical marijuana in the field behind the house. In fact, they had found 1,160 plants on the property with a street value of $4.6 million, along with another 55 pounds of cultivated pot worth about $220,000. "Kimberly, it's the biggest pot bust in this county in the last ten years," he had said. "Kyle could go away for a long time because of this. He really needs to lawyer up. I'm so sorry."

Josie's mom had let out a throaty sigh. "So where is he now?"

"In the lockup. There'll be an arraignment on Monday morning. Because of the seriousness of the charges, I doubt the judge will set bail. So he could be in custody right through a trial."

"And how long could that be?"

"Hard to say with these things. The courts are so back-logged. I mean, we could be talking a year."

Josie had sat slumped on the floor and against the wall listening to the cop. The glee of getting that Tweet from Peter Maxx earlier in the day seemed forever ago, and the happiness she had felt in getting that piano, of sitting on the porch talking to her dad, now all seemed like a farce. How could he be so stupid? How could he keep such a big secret from her?

His jittery paranoia now all made sense. So did his new-found money to afford a piano.

Moreover, the cops had seized every piece of property at the house, including the cell phone she had dropped in the backyard when the officers had rushed the compound. She'd had enough.

> *Fool me once, I say okay*
> *Fool me twice, I can forgive, okay*
> *When it comes to being wronged, third time is no charm*
> *Good-bye to you*

Josie kept replaying the events, over and over. Eventually, though, she fell asleep, and a few hours later she jolted awake, her heart racing and her T-shirt soaked with sweat. She sat up straight and looked around. She gasped when she realized she wasn't inside a jail cell—just a nightmare.

She got up from her bed and flicked on her computer to check the time. It was five o'clock.

Peter. It was almost twenty-four hours since he had sent her that message asking her if she had written any good songs lately. Now was the first moment when she had collected her thoughts enough to reply. That is, assuming it was even him.

How do I know this is you?

But she didn't want to risk offending him. So she added:

The answer to your question is obv yes—I have written a song. Always ☺

17

Peter stood on the front balcony of his house and looked down at the beach. To his left, a half mile away, he saw the Manhattan Beach pier, and to his right up the coast in the far distance he could see the green mountains above the Malibu coast. If there was any material trapping of his success that he appreciated, it was the five-thousand square feet of Spanish-style mansion on the beach that he could afford to relax in.

The fresh salty air, the constant faint sound of waves crashing, the laid-back vibe of the neighborhood. For a boy from Tennessee, it felt like always being on vacation.

In the sand in front of his house was a group of teenagers playing beach volleyball. They were playing guys-versus-girls and laughing the entire time. Peter didn't have a group of local high school friends like those kids. He had his band-mates (but they were all much older), his other TV show cast members (but they all lived up near Hollywood), and, until a few days ago, a girlfriend. Peter often fantasized about what his life would be like if he decided to be a normal teen and enroll in local Mira Costa High School and just give up the celebrity life.

"What's up, kid?"

Dad.

"Just chillin'. Nice to have a day off."

"You're tellin' me. Recharge those batteries of yours. We got eighteen more shows left after Tuesday."

"I know."

"We're down the home stretch." Bobby leaned on the rail beside Peter. "After this tour, we can catch our breath. I think we should do a family vacation. Bora Bora or Cabo or some place like that."

"Or home."

"Nashville? Well, I'm sure Gramma and Grampa would love to see you. We could do that. Sure."

What Bobby failed to mention was that as soon as the tour ended, they were scheduled to release a new single, which Peter would be contractually obligated to promote, launching with the first live performance of this single at the Hot Hollywood Music Awards. Then there was the new season of *For Pete's Sake* that was scheduled to begin taping in late September. Peter computed that would leave them a grand total of six or seven days—max—to "catch their breath."

"Dad, we need to talk about me taking a break soon. Like a real break. I don't want to burn out."

"I get it. I get it." Bobby rubbed the back of his son's neck. "I hear ya. Let's just get through this little bit here."

Bobby fidgeted in his pocket for his car keys. "Look, Petey, I gotta run out to dinner at Fonz's for some Mexican. I'll bring y'all home somethin'. Got it?"

"Got it." Peter continued staring at the high school kids in the sand diving around the volleyball net as his dad walked back inside.

Maybe it was all the oxygenation from his mediation session earlier in the day. Maybe it was having a day off at home and realizing how alone and isolating his life could feel at times like this. Maybe it was he would be turning seventeen in October and was starting to feel the urge to assert his independence, no matter what pressure his dad would put on him to "stay the course" or "keep the eye on the prize" or whatever cliché he spouted to keep Peter on the money-making train. Maybe it was meeting the girl in Bakersfield and sensing the possibility of connecting with a normal life and a normal girl. Whatever the cause of the stirring inside of him, Peter felt different, more alive. He had clarity about what *he* wanted out of his life.

As sunset neared, Peter could see a bank of dark gray clouds a few miles off shore that would be blowing in toward the beach, blanketing the coastline in what the locals called "June gloom." But Peter's view of his life was far from cloudy. In fact, when he walked back inside to his bedroom and looked at his phone and saw the reply message from Josie, he sensed a future as bright as a high-noon sun.

Peter had read the other day that the Earth was inhabited by seven billion people living in 195 different countries, speaking thousands of different languages—from English to Spanish to Mandarin to Japanese to German to Bengali. It got Peter to thinking that more than the Internet, more than television, more than jet travel, more than even Google Translator, there is one thing that shrinks the world and connects all those people more than anything else. It cuts out all the noise, all the distractions, all the worries, all of the madness. And it is the simple act of two strangers discovering each other for the first time. They realize that they aren't alone and that the world is only as big as the space they share between the two of them.

For Peter, it was the chance meeting in a high school classroom and the unrelenting urge he had to talk to Josie again. It was the feeling of wanting to let her into his life, because the more he did, the less alone he would feel. It was like feeling a blanket that was safely wrapped around him.

Josie and Peter were, on paper, very different people from two very different worlds.

But they both were artists, and they both were searching for their blanket.

18

@PeterMaxxNow wow, there you are! I was starting to wonder if I had the wrong address. . . . lol

@MusicLuvr no, just had some dramaz. I'm alive. It's me. PS I can't believe you write "LOL" hahaha

@PeterMaxxNow what's wrong with LOL?

@MusicLuvr nothing. If you are . . . like in your thirties

@PeterMaxxNow I'm an old soul, what can I say . . .

@MusicLuvr BTW, how do I know you are . . . YOU?

@PeterMaxxNow you're right. You don't know if it is ME. Good point. Fair enough.

@MusicLuvr what 2 do, what 2 do . . . LOL

If he was going to get to know this girl, the 140-character constraint of direct-messaging on Twitter wouldn't cut it.

@PeterMaxxNow text me + I can prove it.

Peter sent her his phone number.

@MusicLuvr but I don't have a phone. ☹

@PeterMaxxNow whaaaa? What human being doesn't have a phone?

@MusicLuvr well, I have one. Just lost it.

@PeterMaxxNow do you have IM?

@MusicLuvr **duh. Obv.**

@PeterMaxxNow **screen name?**

@MusicLuvr **josiebrant**

@PeterMaxxNow **brb**

Josie opened up her IM and waited. Not even thirty seconds later, a message popped up on her screen from Peter—or someone claiming to be him. She was 99 percent sure it was him, but she wasn't about to take that for granted just yet.

PETERMAXX: hi josie brant. Hahaha. Just learned ur last name

JOSIEBRANT: yeah, that's me. Now how do I know it's you?

PETERMAXX: take a look.

19

Attached to Peter's IM message was a photo. Josie clicked on it and there was a pic of Peter holding a piece of paper on which he scrawled in black marker, "Hi, Josie Brant. I'm Peter."

Josie squealed. It really was Peter Maxx! And he looked hotter than ever. A two-day scruff of beard and a baseball cap fitted on backward. He wore a plain white T-shirt and was sticking out his tongue playfully.

"Josie, are you okay in there?" her mom shouted through the door, concerned.

"Yes, Mom. I'm fine."

"I thought you were sleeping."

"I woke up, just doing some homework now."

But what she was really doing felt nothing like work.

"Promise me you'll eat something. You haven't eaten since we got home on Friday night."

"Okay, Mom, I will in a bit."

JOSIEBRANT: ok ok. I believe u now

PETERMAXX: I could be an imposter

JOSIEBRANT: true. But I doubt it

PETERMAXX: so howz ur Sunday?

JOSIEBRANT: u don't wanna know

PETERMAXX: yes I do.

JOSIEBRANT: no, u don't

PETERMAXX: I do

JOSIEBRANT: well, my dad's a total freaktard

PETERMAXX: hahaha I can relate

JOSIEBRANT: why r u talking to me? Like shuldnt u be hanging out with famous ppl or something

PETERMAXX: hahahahaha no. I don't like famous people

JOSIEBRANT: well, I don't know any so I cant say.

PETERMAXX: u know me!

JOSIEBRANT: trueski hahahaha

PETERMAXX: I liked meeting you btw

JOSIEBRANT: same

PETERMAXX: u have a nice smile

JOSIEBRANT: same

PETERMAXX: congrats on the contest. Luv ur song.

JOSIEBRANT: tks. Sorry about my friend. She didn't even tell me

PETERMAXX: NP

PETERMAXX: embarrassing u. that's what friends r for huh?

JOSIEBRANT: uggh

JOSIEBRANT: so u just wanted to congrats me?

PETERMAXX: no. well yea. Honestly, IDK. I just thought u were nice and wanted to congratulate u and say hey

JOSIEBRANT: well thank u. cant lie. Im sorta freakin out rt now.

PETERMAXX: hahah. Don't. plz.

JOSIEBRANT: imposs ☺

PETERMAXX: if it makes u feel any better im freaking out now too.

JOSIEBRANT: ?

PETERMAXX: because I never chat with fans like this. I mean, not that ur just a fan.

JOSIEBRANT: well, I AM a fan. But im not crazy, in case ur wondering

PETERMAXX: haha. I know. Btw, I like ur school. Ppl were nice there

JOSIEBRANT: its ok. Last day is tmrow. Then summer vacay! Yay!!

PETERMAXX: nice.

Josie couldn't believe how easy it was to chat with Peter. Everything she had assumed was true about Peter—that he was down-to-Earth, kind, friendly, and really did appreciate his fans—was true. And the computer was an equalizing power. In real life, she barely could put two words together in front of him, but sitting in her bedroom, talking through the keyboard, she felt bolder, more confident. It didn't seem like she was chatting with a pop star. Just a friend. A really *hot* friend. The only guy she had ever rapid-fire chatted so easily with was Christopher, who began IM'ing her in the middle of her chat with Peter.

CHRISTOPHER1: JOSIE ARE YOU OK??? I saw the news. It's everywhere about ur dad.

JOSIEBRANT: Im ok. Sorry. Craziness

CHRISTOPHER1: ive been texting you. Just glad ur ok. I put together a little OLDIES cheer-you-up playlist. ☺

Christopher sent her some links to a new music site he recently discovered that displayed the lyrics sheet and played the song.

JOSIEBRANT: awww sooo sweet of u. will def listen later, my amigo. cops took my phone, dyyyyying w/out it. Ill call ya later. U R the best

CHRISTOPHER1: kk. Im obv here for you if you need ANYTHING.
xo

Josie didn't want to kill Peter's chat buzz, but she couldn't help herself.

JOSIEBRANT: so does sandy know ur chatting w me. Wouldn't she be jealz?

PETERMAXX: she definitely would be jealy. But we broke up.

If it weren't so uncool to do so, Josie would have written "OMG" a million times. But she didn't. The last thing she wanted to seem like was desperate.

JOSIEBRANT: sorry to hear that. I hate when people feed me jealy sandwiches.

PETERMAXX: NP. it's for the best. cant believe im telling u all this btw . . . !

JOSIEBRANT: why r u?

PETERMAXX: this pbly sounds weird but I trust u.

JOSIEBRANT: well, im glad you are. FYI: I AM a trustworthy person.

PETERMAXX: good. Had that feeling. Now I have a quesht for you . . .

JOSIEBRANT: okayyyy . . .

PETERMAXX: how old are you?

JOSIEBRANT: gonna be 15 in 3 weeks.

PETERMAXX: so then . . . if my math is correct that makes you 14! hahaha!!!

JOSIEBRANT: technically yes.

PETERMAXX: well, my dad says "age is just a number."

JOSIEBRANT: so true Mr. 16!! haha

PETERMAXX: true Mrs. "Almost 15"

JOSIEBRANT: LMFAO

PETERMAXX: so, like, we are off the record, right??

JOSIEBRANT: YES

PETERMAXX: phew. Good. U can keep this chat our little secret?

JOSIEBRANT: duh

PETERMAXX: not tell any1 we r friends . . . i mean, chat buddies . . . ?

JOSIEBRANT: duh, secret pals.

PETERMAXX: :)

PETERMAXX: ugh. My dad's buggin. Dinnertime. so when u find a phone u can text me ok? I'm not on the laptop very much.

JOSIEBRANT: YES! perf

PETERMAXX: Sweet. Gnite, josiebrant.

JOSIEBRANT: Gnite, petermaxx.

Josie stood up and looked down at her trembling hands. She walked over to the mirror and saw those nervous red splotches all over her face. She wanted to scream. She wanted to run and tell her mom—tell the world!—what just happened. She wished she could Tweet her fifty-nine followers the news. #Winning!

Instead she made a phone call.

"Hello?"

"Ash. It's Josie."

"Oh my god, Josie. Where are you? Everyone has been freaking out! Did you see the news? It is everywhere. Like everywhere and stuff. The rumor was that you were in jail. What's this phone number?"

"I'm home," Josie whispered. "Cops took my cell. I am totally freaking out right now."

"What's gonna happen? Are you in trouble?"

"No, just my dad. None of us knew what he was doing. But my mom said we're not supposed to talk about it. It's a legal thing. But can I ask you a favor-ski?"

"Okay."

"Do you still have that old-school phone you used to use before you got the iPhone? I could really use it. I was thinking maybe I could borrow it until the cops give mine back."

Ashley didn't immediately respond. After a few seconds, Josie began thinking the phone had gone dead. "Ash, you there?"

"I'm here, but, Josie, I have to tell you something."

"If it's about the contest thing, it's cool. I was mad, but now I'm over it. I know your heart was in the right place. I mean, we are besties and nothing ever could—"

"No, Josie, not about the contest," Ashley interrupted. "It's my parents. They saw the news about your dad. They told me I'm not allowed to talk to you anymore."

Josie had been pacing her room. Now she stood still. "What? Why?"

"You know, the drugs, your dad, the whole thing. They're superstrict and . . ."

"Ashley, what are you talking about?" Josie would have cried if she had any tears left, but they were all dried into the grass in her dad's front yard and soaked into tissues back at the police station. "I've known you since kindergarten. We are BFFs. Your parents know the real me. I didn't do anything wrong. The cops even said I was just a victim of circumstance. The truth will come out."

"I'm sorry, Josie. I should go. My mom will kill me if she knows I'm even talking to you. They went through my phone last night looking at messages. They don't trust you. I'm so sorry but—"

"No, Ashley, really. Look, I can explain to them that . . ."

"I gotta go, Josie. I'll talk to ya later. Bye."

"Wait, Ashley, no—"

Silence.

Dial tone.

20

"Hey, guys. I'm Peter Maxx. Join me and all your favorite music stars on August twenty-eighth for the Hot Hollywood Music Awards. Because if it's not hot, it's not Hot Hollywood."

"And . . . cut!"

The director, a chubby, bearded guy in his forties who waved his hands dramatically with every word, got up from his chair and walked toward Peter, who was standing in front of a green screen.

"Can we try it again, Peter? But, this time, give us a big, Peter Maxx smile? That will give it a nice, big punch for the fans."

The director sat down in his chair beside the camera and watched the makeup artist dab Peter's forehead with some anti-shine powder.

"Can we give him a little more color?" the director asked the makeup girl. "More bronzer. On the cheeks."

Peter rolled his eyes and glared at his dad, who sat next to Abby sipping from a white paper coffee cup watching the video monitor. Bobby flicked his son an enthusiastic thumbs-up. Peter flashed an obnoxiously fake smile back at him.

Although the Hot Hollywood Awards weren't for another three months, Peter was already shooting promos; his concert tour, just into the second half, would wrap a few days before the awards show. In fact, right after wrapping the shoot he was scheduled to hop a jet for Kansas City.

Peter felt silly reading the insipid script off the Prompter, especially the cheesy last line, but it was part of the game. The Hot Hollywood execs were so pleased with how the "Sing It to the Maxx" contest went that his dad and Abby had struck a deal with them to let Peter world premiere his new single on their high-rated awards show. It was the biggest night in pop music every year. To debut a new song with a live performance on the show usually resulted in the song being the number-one downloaded song the next day. Being the opening act was pop music gold. Peter's lack of shared enthusiasm with his dad had nothing to do with him not appreciating the opportunity— because he did. Peter just didn't like the song he was set to sing that night: a romantic duet with Sandy.

Peter dutifully performed a few more takes before leaving the soundstage in West L.A. and heading for LAX with his dad, Big Jim, and Abby for a hectic week that would start Tuesday in Kansas City and end in Las Vegas on Saturday night. In the limo, Peter turned on his phone, checking if Josie had yet entered the twenty-first century and texted him yet. She hadn't. But it was only noon. There was still hope.

Abby used the car time to brief Peter on his media hits. The reviews of the Oakland show were amazing, she explained, with 95 percent of them rated as "positive" by her PR agency.

"What do the other five percent say they didn't like?" Bobby asked.

Abby scrolled through the reviews on her tablet. "Looks like the usual, mostly complaints that Peter doesn't bring enough energy to his hits."

"Greeeeat." Peter groaned.

"But they're the minority," Abby said. "Most everyone loved it."

"Son, you remember what Ricky Nelson sang, right?" Bobby weighed in from the front seat. "You can't please everyone, so . . ."

"I know, I know: *please yourself*," Peter finished.

"Exactamundo," Bobby said.

Abby handed him a press release. "It hits stores tomorrow, and we need you to approve this today."

Peter Maxx has created a perfume for the girls who love him. The fragrance is called "Special" and a portion of the proceeds from sales of the fragrance will go toward pediatric cancer research. Retailing for $45 a bottle, "Special" hits stores nationwide on Tuesday. Peter Maxx says of his latest brand extension: "Let's face it, the way a girl smells is something that is very important, very special to a guy. I have a deep connection with my fans, and creating a fragrance that I personally love is another way I can bring them closer to me."

"Fine, whatever." He handed it back to Abby and shook his head in disgust. "Hey, Dad. Why didn't anyone tell me about this perfume launch thing?"

"We just did," he said harshly.

Abby nervously sat beside Peter and pretended to read her phone.

A few minutes from LAX, Abby broke the awkward silence and continued to rush through her publicity report.

"Oh, and saving the best for last," she added. "OMC is asking for comment on this story they posted today." She showed Peter the blog post, with the headline: "Peter Maxx Getting Married—Source Says." It quoted a "source close to Peter" as saying Peter and Sandy were so in love that he had recently told her they would get married after their summer concert tour.

"Now that's funny," Peter said. "Where do they get these so-called 'sources'?"

"So there's nothing I should know about?" Bobby cracked.

"No, Dad. I am definitely not getting married."

Peter still hadn't broken the news to his dad that he and Sandy had split. He was waiting for the right time and, well, he was too tired to have to endure his dad's motormouth chattering over how to spin the split and, most important, what to do about the duet. Maybe, Peter thought, he would from now on treat his dad like he was treated, like with the fragrance launch: On a "need-to-know basis."

OMC, short for "Oh My Celebrity," had no shame to their game. There was no story too nasty or mean for them to run for the self-promoted "#1 Source for Celebrity Sleaze." The site even had an e-mail address where "tipsters" could anonymously send in information that fell within the tabloid holy trinity of hookups, breakups, and screw-ups.

Some of the tips were true. Some, like the Peter-Sandy marriage story, were total fiction. It was the job of OMC news desk editors to figure it out, and when they couldn't, they would throw a story up crediting a "source"—even if they had no way of proving the story. As OMC's British-born Editor-in-Chief Johnny Love said, "I don't care about the facts. Give me the gossip!"

OMC readers would click on anything Peter Maxx, so much that they had begun a branded blog post they cheekily called "Your Daily Peter." It was consistently the site's number-one read item every day. Even if it was total garbage.

"So I will tell OMC you are not getting married?" Abby said.

"No, just say no comment. Don't give them the satisfaction of an actual comment. I will just Tweet that it's crap."

On the plane, Peter sunk into his leather seat and typed out a Tweet on his phone.

@PeterMaxxNow for those of you wondering, I am not getting married. Don't let the facts get in the way of a good story @OMC.

As the plane door was about to close, he got a text from a 661 area code.

hey 16. It's Almost 15.

Peter's mood instantly lightened.

P—hey josiebrant. I c u got a phone. Niiice.

J—yup. My friend saved the day!

P—Im literally on the plane, about to takeoff. Text ya later! Something I really want to ask u!!

J—what?!

Ten seconds later . . .

J—Um . . .

Ten more seconds later . . .

J—r u really gonna leave a girl hangin?

21

"Josie, what's wrong?" Christopher asked. "You all good?"

Josie had been texting furiously in front of Christopher in her living room. Literally two seconds after he handed her his phone, she began texting Peter.

It was a Monday, the last day of school before summer break. Josie, embarrassed to walk the halls of Lawndale High with everyone whispering behind her back, stayed home. Christopher came by with the phone right after school let out and had been quietly checking Facebook on his phone while she texted. But, like any sane human being, he grew worried when she started grunting and huffing and puffing at it as if it were a really annoying (not to mention, tiny) person in the palm of her hand.

"Is it the phone?" Christopher asked. "If it's dying, I'm really sorry. It's a piece of junk, and the battery dies easily, so . . ."

"No, the phone's fine." Josie still stared at the tiny screen. "I'm just frustrated. It's okay."

"Is it your dad?" he asked.

"No, no, not my dad," Josie said, clutching the tiny cell like it was glued to her palm. "He can't text in jail. And that's the way it is gonna be a for long time."

"How long?"

"Well, my mom went to his arraignment today and the judge set bail at five million dollars." Josie glanced down at her phone. "So, basically, he's in jail until his trial, which could be like next year. So, like, I won't see him forever. I'm most worried about Connor. I'll be fine. But he's pretty freaked out. Whatever."

Christopher looked at Josie in an affectionate kind of way that a boyfriend might, and she noticed. As he reached to touch her knee, Josie crossed her leg to keep him from touching her.

He pulled his hand away in an awkward silence.

"How much did you say your dad's bail amount is?"

Josie was relieved he changed the subject.

"Five million," she answered with a sigh.

"So if he pays five million dollars he can go free for now?"

Josie let out a breath. Make that half a breath. Her tight chest couldn't relax enough to release all the air pent up behind her ribs.

"No. Mom said a bail bondsman or someone like that would post up the money if we could come up with ten percent of that as, like, a down payment."

"So, really, you only need $500,000 then."

"Yeah, only *half* a million."

Josie buried her face in her phone and texted as she talked. "Christopher, it's not worth talking about. My family is broke, and your mom can't even afford to give you an allowance. It's not like Bakersfield is filled with rich people who will pay it. Especially because they don't want people to think they are connected to a drug dealer."

"Farmer," Christopher corrected Josie. "He was farming."

"Whatever. He is like a total pariah now. And, by association, so am I, and it totally sucks. He should just rot in jail."

"So you can't even, like, go and visit your dad?"

"No, you gotta be eighteen. So, poor me, I'm not allowed to go to jail and talk to my shackled dad through glass. Poor, poor me."

Josie began laughing—but more like a hobo on a street corner than an ironic, bemused teenager.

"Who are you texting, by the way?" Christopher asked.

"Me?"

"No, the little green man sitting next to you on the couch."

Josie had promised Peter she wouldn't tell anyone about their friendship, even her closest friends. Plus, she assumed Christopher would just cop her a bad attitude and remind her how lame Peter's music was.

"Just my mom," Josie lied.

Maybe she used to feel guilty when she didn't tell the truth. In the past, she would always share everything with Christopher. But now, everyone and everything in Bakersfield annoyed her. Her secret connection with Peter was her escape from all the stress, all the eyes on her now that her dad was in jail. She knew what kids at school were saying. She saw the Facebook comments of kids gossiping about her being a pothead—not to mention about her being so "desperate" for attention she flirted with Peter Maxx in front of the cameras.

"Did you listen to the mix I sent you?" Christopher said. "Maybe that will cheer you up."

"I haven't. If I thought it would erase all the crap that's happened to me in the last three days I would have listened. But the last time I checked your mix isn't capable of doing that."

Christopher got up and grabbed his backpack. "I better get going. Obviously, I'm not making you feel any better. When Josie *Brat* is gone, tell Josie *Brant* she should text me. I'll be waiting for her."

Christopher stormed out the door before Josie could come back with an equally sarcastic retort. Regardless, Josie wasn't so sure she cared. There was only one person she felt like talking to, and it wasn't anyone in Bakersfield. Although the city had 350,000 people and was the ninth largest in California, those statistics were deceiving. Josie's world was a very small one. Just about everyone used to think she was a freak, and now, with her dad's shady farming, she was sure any remaining doubters had come to conclude the same thing.

If one could suffer claustrophobia just from living in a small town, she was feeling that. She needed to breathe, to get away. But to where? She was stuck. The only person she knew who didn't live in Bakersfield was Peter, and, well, she didn't exactly *know* him that well at all.

As Josie sat on her living room sofa, five minutes had

passed since Peter's last text. She assumed he had turned off his phone and she would have to wait for a few hours before hearing from him.

> *A watched pot never boils*
> *A watched phone never rings*
> *When you're feeling so low why's life so full of such*
>> *frustrating things?*

22

Peter's jet took off and banked north over the Pacific coastline. A few minutes later, high above the rugged brown San Gabriel mountains east of L.A. and heading east on a straight shot to Kansas City, he looked down at the valley that opened up to the north—the valley where Bakersfield sat at the southernmost tip, an average little city with a not-so-average girl.

Peter didn't write many songs anymore. Starting out, he and his dad would write songs together all the time. But, nowadays, he was given songs by various producers and writers—so many, in fact, that he just had to decide which ones he wanted.

Most of Peter's recent hits were actually written by the producing/songwriting duo known as Tempo Team. The producers that comprised the team were Kara Cox and Mark Lemon, a hip couple in their thirties who lived and worked out of a home studio in Santa Monica. They had been on an unprecedented hit-making run, with fourteen top ten hits in the last two years—five of them with Peter.

Everyone wanted to work with Tempo Team, as doing so was tantamount to being delivered a fat lottery check. Right before he left for tour, Peter's label paid top dollar to have him work with Tempo Team, and they were the ones who came up with the lyrics for his duet with Sandy. Peter's fans assumed

Peter truly collaborated with them on all his songs, but the truth was that more often than not, he was handed a lyric sheet and sang from it, maybe changing a word here and there. Still, Peter got a shared songwriting credit on each song due to the legal definition of writing a song. In fact, the guys at Tempo Team had a saying about working with Peter. "Say a word, get a third."

Peter didn't feel right taking credit for someone else's songs, but his father insisted that this was "the way it works." And, by the way, he added, "Never look a gift horse in the mouth." If Tempo Team was delivering the hits, Peter was the face and voice of them. Songwriting and producing being a collaborative process, this was just the system of making hits.

Even so, Peter wanted to write his own music. He wanted to stop the lie. Josie's songwriting talent only convinced him of this more.

As the plane scraped across the blue sky, Peter scribbled words onto a napkin. They flowed like water down a stream. He didn't have to think. He just had to transcribe his brain.

"Whatchya doin over there, Son?" his dad asked from across the aisle, somewhere over the Nevada desert.

"Writing," he replied, then returning to strumming his acoustic guitar in between scribbling on the napkin.

"You got yourself a hit there, do ya?"

"I don't know, maybe," Peter said, red-faced with embarrassment. "Just writing. Maybe I'll perform it. We'll see."

"Writing is good for the soul. And the wallet. Keep it up."

A half hour later, Peter put his pen down and guitar back in its case. The roar of the engines lulled him into a meditative state as he looked over at his dad dozing off in his reclined seat.

"Hey, Dad."

"Huh?"

"Can I ask you something?"

"Ask away," he said gruffly.

"Why am I launching this stupid perfume? I mean, whose idea was that?"

"First of all, it's a fragrance, not a perfume," Bobby said, his eyes fuming. "Every big star has one. Beyoncé, J Lo, Bieber. They've all done it. It's another way to connect with fans. Another revenue stream."

"But I don't even like perfume," he said deliberately. "I mean, fragrance."

Bobby sat up and rubbed his blood-shot eyes and scratched his graying goatee, then unbuckled his seat belt and walked over to Peter's seat. He settled down beside his son.

"Look, Son," Bobby said, resting his hand on Peter's knee. "It's a licensing deal and they're paying you a pretty penny for it. Two mill to be exact. And that's guaranteed up front, before a single bottle is sold. Don't make me out to be some big bad wolf. You can get off this train anytime you want. No one is making you do this. Any of this. But you need to know that once you hop off, there ain't no guarantee you can ever get back on."

Bobby twisted the silver wedding band on his right ring finger.

"And, trust me, if anyone knows this, it's me. When I walked away from the business, I thought, 'Aw, heck. I'll just take some time off and it will all be waiting for me when I get back.' Well, it wasn't. This business moves fast. Tastes change. The next Bobby, the next Peter, the next big, hot singer comes up and, well, people move on. You gotta strike while the iron is hot."

Peter had heard all this too many times to count. He stared out the window down at the green, quilt-like patches of Midwestern farmland.

"That's why," Bobby continued, "as long as you're playing the game, you do everything to score as many points as you can before the clock ticks down to zero. Because it will. It may seem like your fans will always be there, always wanna spend forty bucks for a T-shirt and five hundred bucks to get a picture with you. But they won't. So if you want me to go back to Abby and tell her to tear up that press release. If you want me to cancel all the deals we have in place. Heck, if you want me to cancel the rest of the tour, I'll do it. But I just want you to know that if you do, you would seriously be pissing away everything we've worked so hard for, everything that your mom would have been so proud of us for achieving."

Peter faced his father. "Mom?"

"Yeah. Mom. She would be so proud."

"I think Mom would be happy just knowing I'm happy. I don't think Mom would care how much money I was making off selling perfume to little girls. She would just want me to be happy."

Bobby's left leg started twitching. He stuck it out into the aisle and kicked his foot up and down as if on a bass drum pedal.

"Well, I ain't disagreeing with ya, but exactly what about all of this . . ." Bobby threw his hands up and pointed at the private jet cabin, gesturing toward the attractive female flight attendant in the tight-fitting blue dress preparing lunch in the front. "What about all this doesn't make you happy? I'm trying to think what I can do to make you any happier. I mean, the truth is that you're treated like a king."

"Maybe I don't want to be a king," Peter said defiantly.

"Don't want to be a king?" Bobby raised his voice an octave. "Where I come from, if you don't want to be treated like a king, then, well, heck, you're more nuts than a peanut factory."

The jet suddenly hit a pocket of turbulence, bouncing them both up out of their seats. Bobby, already a nervous flyer, snapped on his seat belt and pulled it tight across his lap.

"Tell me. Just how do you wanna be treated?" Bobby asked.

Peter shrugged his shoulders. If he would have given it more thought, he probably would have come up with a different answer, something more rehearsed. But he didn't. Instead, he looked at his dad and, for the first time in a very long time, told his father exactly what was on his mind and said, "Like a kid."

23

Friends or lovers
I need to know
On text, it's like we're unpeeling
The onion of our connection
I hope he doesn't add to my
*   heartbreak collection*

Josie kept writing. The song kept coming to her. She hummed them quietly on her bed as she scribbled them into her diary.

What did he mean, "text ya later"
What's he gonna ask next?
Does he want to know my favorite color
Or if I'll be his lover

Josie was starting to realize that if she was just getting to know a boy from, say, her geometry class, it would be easy to conduct background research. She could ask his friends, stalk him on Facebook, talk to her friends who know him—all in an effort to discern whether he liked her, like-liked her, or if he was just bored and flirting with her for sport and would crush her little heart like a grape.

But the normal rules couldn't be applied in this case. Her newfound friend was a global pop superstar, all the usual getting-to-know-you rules were thrown out the door. They didn't go to the same school. In fact, he didn't even go to high school! They had no friends in common, unless she suddenly became incredibly dialed into the exclusive fraternity of global pop superstars. And since he was so adored and lusted after by millions of girls all around the world, she couldn't help but feel totally insecure, not to mention unconfident in her chances of Peter being into her—*only* her. Even if he was sweet on text. Even if she felt a special connection when they first met. Even if he was the one who had Tweeted her first. Even if he had given her nothing to assume he wasn't into her.

Josie checked Peter's Twitter, his Facebook, the celebrity blogs. Searching for clues. Looking to find out if there were any secret messages. Looking to see if, maybe, she could catch him in a lie. And her obsessive surfing eventually took her to the home page of *Oh My Celebrity* where the top-line story declared that Peter Maxx was "getting married" to his longtime girlfriend Sandy, the very gorgeous blond singer whom he had texted to Josie yesterday that he had broken up with.

And just when Josie was about to get so depressed she could speed-dial the suicide hotline, she checked his Twitter and read his denial: "For those of you wondering, I am not getting married." Then for now, she could breathe a sigh of relief, because there was still a chance, however minor, that, as crazy as it would sound if she ever said this to anyone, she could be the one to marry him. Someday.

But he still hadn't texted her back.

And while she fantasized about the possibilities—because

it was a hell of a lot more fun than thinking about her dad being in jail, or her friends abandoning her, or facing a summer of being bored—she wrote songs. Because it was all she had ever done to sort through the maze of emotions that was her life.

> People talking behind your back
> You're under attack
> All alone
> Such a small town
> Holding you down

She wrote so much into the night that she fell asleep with a pen in her hand. The next morning, she popped awake at six o'clock, a Tuesday. She had committed his tour schedule to memory, so she knew he was in Kansas City and that he was two time zones ahead. But when she checked her phone with her bleary eyes, she saw that he still hadn't texted. She collapsed onto her pillow and fell back asleep.

Three hours later, Josie woke up to a knock on her door. Her first day of summer vacation, and she was feeling exhausted. She pressed a pillow over her head.

Through the door, as usual, her mom shouted that her father might call anytime between now and noon, that these were his hours he would have access to a jail house phone, and he wanted to talk to her.

"Whatever," Josie snipped at her mom before slipping out the front door, grabbing a pen, her tattered spiral songwriting notebook, and, naturally, her cell phone just in case the text she had been awaiting for the last nineteen hours (but, really, who's counting?) entered her screen and made her life complete.

She walked the mile to the strip mall and sat down at Starbucks. She began to write and think (and obsessively check her phone) and watch other kids her age hanging out with their parents being all normal and stuff, while she sat alone and cheered herself up with thoughts like, "Hey, at least I'm not fourteen and pregnant!"

An hour passed, then another hour, and just when she was thinking another iced sugar-free caramel soy latte would be a bad idea for her heart, her phone vibrated to life on the table.

Your dad called and you are NOT here.

Josie smiled devilishly because, maybe, now she made someone who hurt her also feel hurt. And, while she was smart and compassionate and mature enough to know that this was not a very healthy thought, she couldn't help but feel good about the very bad thing she had just done.

*If I pick up the phone it will be
to remind you
Of the mess you left when you got
locked away
Your burden, I give back to you*

But then on her walk of shame back home Josie started feeling like a jerk, like she was only making things worse. She didn't want to be the kind of cynical kid that moped around

Lawndale High, drinking her Haterade, wearing her cynicism as an armor protecting herself from the reality that she wasn't quite as smart or cool as she wished.

In fact, being the anticynic was Josie's religion, and the resulting songs comprised her personal Bible, especially ever since she read that quote from her TV hero Conan O'Brien after NBC fired him: "I hate cynicism—it's my least favorite quality and it doesn't lead anywhere. Nobody in life gets exactly what they thought they were going to get. But if you work really hard and you're kind, amazing things will happen."

Josie had taped that quote to her bedroom wall for inspiration and had read it almost every day since. She had read it aloud so many times that it seemed like due karma when, finally, something truly amazing happened. For the first time in her life, she felt like she was living a dream, and it began with a vibration in the back pocket of her shorts.

She stopped on the sidewalk along the busy boulevard and pulled out the phone and, suddenly, the emotional roller coaster that had been her life for the last few days shot back up to the top, where the view seemed to go on forever.

Peter's text was not just a mere message, not just another flirty little zap across the digital grid. It was an apology for being "so busy," and then an explanation of why he took a day to get back—that he was just busy being a global pop superstar.

And then came the part that is so *Cinderella*, so beyond anything that she expected, that Josie would spend the next two days just rereading it over and over again: An invite, a request of her presence in Las Vegas in just three days.

> I've been thinking a lot about you. I want to write
> songs with you, talk about life. . . . I want u to c my
> concert and just hang out.

She never felt so wanted, so attractive, so loved as the moment after she texted back, "Yes!" and, then again, when he immediately replied, "See u then! ☺."

Suddenly, the biggest drama in her life was not wondering if her dad was going to prison for life, or if the entire city of Bakersfield would shun her, but rather it was figuring out how a fourteen-year-old girl best informs her mom she's off to Vegas.

After much thought, the answer was obvious: A fourteen-year-old girl never in a million years tells her mom such a thing. No mom in her right mind would allow their teen daughter to go off to Sin City to meet up with an older boy.

So Josie began to scheme and plot and figure out how she could get what she wanted, and, like a lot of things in her life lately, it started with a text.

> J—hey, Delilah. Ive got an idea to run by ya.

> > D—if it involves that cheerleader bitch again,
> > Im SO not down.

> J—it doesnt. Dont worry, D.

> > D—so . . .

> J—ever been to Vegas? Wanna come with?

> > D—meet me at the hot tub at six.

24

When Josie stepped through the front door of her apartment, her mom stood ready for battle.

Her nose red apparently from blowing it, Josie's mom announced, "Your dad was really disappointed you weren't home when he called."

Not even slipped out of her shoes, Josie shot back, "Okay, well, I'm really disappointed he's ruined my life."

"Everyone makes mistakes. You need to learn how to forgive. You only have one father."

"And he has one daughter," Josie snapped, stomping down the hallway.

"You're not running away this time!"

Her mom's firm occupational therapist–strong grip grabbed her bicep. Tears were now streaming down both their cheeks.

"Look, Josie. Forgiving is not the same as forgetting. But forgiving will at least help you let go of the pain. You don't think I've forgotten all the drunk nights I spent with your dad, do you? Wondering if he would come home, and if he did whether it would be happy Kyle or angry Kyle. Of course, I remember those nights. Every single one of them. But, you know what, Josie? I have forgiven him. That's called moving on. That's called healing. You? You're just running away."

Josie exploded into a crumble of sobbing, burying her face in the soft shoulder of her mom, who rubbed her back and softly said, "I don't want to see you in so much pain. It hurts me and it hurts you."

"I don't know if I can forgive him," Josie said. "I just don't know."

Josie released from her mom's squishy, loving embrace, wiped her tears with her sleeve and continued walking toward her bedroom and shut the door.

When she sat down in her desk chair her eyes found that favorite Conan O'Brien quote and she realized that Conan was right. Yet he also wasn't about to turn fifteen in less than a week. She sat there thinking that she had never left the state of California, never done anything that could remotely fit the definition of being independent, of being an adult. That quote spoke to her in a way that it had never done before. It read like something a parent tells a kid when they want you to just settle for what they want—not what you want.

It came to her like a news flash: she was turning fifteen and had never had a real boyfriend! Another news flash: she'd been on a few dates, had a crush on one boy, shared a short kiss on the lips at her last middle-school dance, but she had never even, officially, made out!

It was time. Time to grow up, and away, from her mom— her constant questioning, trying to control her, snooping through her phone, cuddling her like she was a kindergartner.

25

Josie had long ago concluded that the hot tub was the only cool thing about living at the Mountainview Apartments, a collection of '80s-era, two-story stucco buildings. The rectangular buildings had the color of oatmeal and, frankly, the place could use a fresh coat of paint.

Josie slipped into her favorite two-piece black bikini; she imagined Peter seeing her in it at the pool in Vegas. She smeared on some bright-red lipstick and flat-ironed her hair into wavy curls that cascaded down onto her chest like a celebrity. She pictured the paparazzi taking pictures of her as she put her big feet into a pair of heels and looked at herself in the mirror.

"Ugh, stripper," Josie observed aloud, putting on sandals instead.

When she walked down to the hot tub, she found Delilah already sitting on the edge, waiting for her. Delilah was eighteen and looked like it, filling in her neon-yellow bikini like a woman that Josie was not quite yet.

"You said Vegas, Brant?" D kicked her feet in the water. "Vegas? Really?"

"Yes," Josie replied. "Vegas."

"What makes you think a girl like me would ever want to

go to Vegas?"

"Because you're the only person I know who is always up for an adventure."

Delilah nodded. "True, Brant. Very true."

"And you're the only person I know who might be willing to drive us there."

"True. But, like, have you ever heard of a bus? I'm not running a limo service."

Josie settled slowly into the bubbling tub across from D. "Ever since those college kids were stabbed on the bus last year, I'm not allowed to ride a bus."

D threw her head back and laughed. "So you're telling me that you aren't allowed to take a bus, but your mom wouldn't care that you're hitching a ride with your shady neighbor?"

"You're not shady."

"I didn't say I was. I'm saying your mom thinks I'm shady."

"Well, yeah, she does. But, honestly, it's not her. To me, the bus is gross and for real sketch. As long as you don't drive like a nut, then I feel safer with you. Plus I need a partner in crime."

Delilah slid her womanly body down so the water came up to just below her chin.

"Why Vegas?" D asked.

"If I tell you, you can't tell anyone," Josie whispered. Josie scanned the hot tub area with paranoid eyes. "It is, like, beyond a secret."

"Okay fine. Secret. Just tell me."

"To see a boy."

"Well, obviously. It always is. And you're right. This so needs to be a secret. Especially because your mom thinks you're a little Goody Two-shoes."

"What do you mean by that?"

"Are you kidding me?" D said. "Like, seriously, Brant, your mom thinks you've got Barbie private parts!"

"Huh?" Josie asked, confused.

"I mean, she thinks you don't have a sexual bone in your body. And, no offense, neither did I until just now. Not that I'm complaining. I kinda like it."

Josie's cheeks turned red, and not just because of the 102-degree water.

"So when is this sketch rendezvous of yours supposed to happen?"

"Well, the boy says I should come on Friday afternoon. We'd have to drive back Sunday morning."

"Interesting." Delilah dipped her long black hair back into the steaming tub. Squeezing it dry with both her hands, she added, "What's gonna be your cover?"

"My what?"

"You know, like your cover story. Like, what is the fake story you're telling your mom to explain where you will be for like forty-eight hours?"

"Oh, right." Josie hesitated. "Well, I was gonna tell her that, um, I was having a sleepover at a friend's house or something."

"You better come up with something better than that, kid!"

Slumping into the tub, Josie blew bubbles in deep thought for a moment.

"Wait!" She bolted upright. "This coming weekend is Ashley's Sweet Sixteen camping birthday at Lake Isabella."

"And . . ."

"And, well, I will just tell my mom that's where I'm going."

"Genius," D said approvingly. "Just one problem: I'm flat broke, Brant. I've got like zero money for gas. It will be like a hundred bucks for gas. Plus I have to work at the restaurant on Saturday. I'd probably make a hundred bucks, so I'd be losing that. Then there's the hotel . . ."

"The hotel is totes gonna be free," Josie assured her.

"Who is this dude? Some sort of sugar daddy?"

"No!"

"Okay. Tell me who."

"I can't. I promised him I wouldn't."

"Here's the deal." Delilah got up out of the hot tub and adjusted her top. "You don't tell me, then I don't take you."

"Okay, okay," Josie said in a hushed voice. "It's Peter Maxx."

"Get out. Get the F out."

Josie got out of the tub and grabbed her phone. She showed the text from Peter:

> I'll put you up in a suite at the Palazzo. Everything will be taken care of. Will be funnnnn. Come. Friday.

Delilah's eyes popped open wider than the Gulf of Mexico.

"I always knew there was a bad girl lurking inside that good girl exterior just wanting to get out."

"Totes," Josie said with a smile, settling back into the tub.

"Brant. If you can come up with a hundred bucks for gas, I'm in. I think it could be epic. Sexy. So just lemme know."

Before opening the pool gate and leaving, D told her student, "Just promise me you will stop saying 'totes.'"

Self-satisfied, Josie rested the back of her head on the tub's concrete edge and stared up at the clear blue sky. A few minutes later, the jets timed out and she could see her skinny, pale thighs, and the first thing that came to mind was how much she really was going to need a tan . . . that was, if she could scheme up a way to come up with a hundred bucks. She remembered that she still had that twenty-five bucks that her dad gave her last week for groceries but never spent. So, if her calculations were accurate, all she needed, really, was seventy-five dollars.

When she got back to her apartment and her mom was waiting in the living room to greet her and hug her again and say she was sorry for being so harsh earlier, Josie sweetly hugged her and told her it was okay, that she knew she was just being a good mom, looking out for her.

Then, before walking into her room so she could excitedly start texting with her gorgeous boy crush, she flashed the most innocent doe eyes and reminded her mom that this weekend was her BFF Ashley's camping weekend up in the mountains and—gee golly gosh-oh-gosh—how much she was looking forward to just getting away and being with her friends.

"Oh, honey," her mom cooed. "Of course you do."

That's when Josie went to hit the golf ball that she had just so manipulatively set on the tee: "But can I borrow fifty bucks to buy a present for her? She's been such a good friend to me; I would die without her." Josie flashed the doe eyes again. "And, oh, I also need like twenty-five bucks to buy some camping supplies, food, and stuff."

After her mom promised to leave a check on the counter in the morning, after Josie hit that perfectly teed-up ball smack down the middle of the Mommy fairway, she texted D.

> J—got the hundy.
>
> D—sexy.
>
> J—so noon Friday?
>
> D—yup. Noon it is.

It was seven o'clock, and, even though she knew that Peter was set to go onstage in Kansas City at eight, she texted him anyway, because at least he might see the text when he got offstage.

> so, good news. Im in!! I can go. See you Friday.

Then she clicked on her Peter Maxx playlist and on came his hit "Like We Rock."

> *Shake you, take you*
> *As you are*

Make you, never break you
That's who we are
Like we rock. . . .

Josie stood in front of the mirror listening to what was by far his sexiest song, brushing her wet hair and puckering her lips and singing along. She cocked her hips to the side like a supermodel at a photo shoot and wondered if this was what it felt like to be not a girl, but a woman.

26

Peter and his dad were arguing—again.

After their midflight spat on the way to Kansas City, they hugged it out over dinner later that night. Peter apologized and Bobby suggested that the stress and strain was natural—and expected. Forty-city tours were hard on experienced performers, so of course a sixteen-year-old performer would have his moments of cracking. They both agreed that Peter being happy was most important and the last couple days went on as planned. Strong as oak, Bobby promised.

A day later, in the dressing room at the Sprint Center, they were back to battling.

"Your fans don't want acoustics, Son. Well, maybe like one or two a night to slow it down, pace your set out. But mostly they want you to rock. They want bass and drums. They want to feel the energy in their bodies. They wanna dance. That's why they come out to see you live. And they want to hear your hits and have fun—not hear some drippy folk song you wrote on a napkin."

"But they also have the Web and know my set playlist better than I do. I just want to mix it up. This isn't the '90s, Dad. You gotta stay ahead of the fans. I don't want to be so predictable. They deserve to see a different kind of show every night."

Bobby was shaking his head and if he went a few seconds more without inhaling Peter was convinced steam would start puffing from his ears and nostrils.

"Trust me, Peter. Sappy doesn't work for you. Look what it did to *my* career!"

"Don't start in with that, Dad," Peter demanded.

"With what?"

"With your do-what-I-say-or-be-washed-up-like-me BS."

Just as Bobby was about to argue, all five of the G Girls, with Sandy leading the pack, ran by them in their skimpy girl-group getups. Sandy high-fived Peter, then Bobby. They offered a lifeless high-five back to each of the girls as they disappeared down the hall.

"That's just not realistic, Peter," Bobby continued, a little less riled up. "We can't crank out a different show every night. Name one band that does that. Okay, the Grateful Dead used to, but besides them—no one. No one! You want me to go tell your musical director you want a different set list every night and we have to rehearse with the lighting crew, the sound guys, the backup singers, the band, everyone. We have a formula for a reason."

"Dad, it's one freakin' song. That's all I'm saying. I just want to play one song. I don't need the band. All I need is my acoustic guitar and one light on me."

"Fine," Bobby said. "I hear ya. Loud and clear. You want to do your own thing. It will make you 'happy' blah-blah-blah. Wish granted."

Bobby grabbed his earplugs from his front pocket. "But not tonight, Son. I want you to rehearse it first. Maybe in a few days. Maybe in Vegas."

"I want to play it in Vegas."

"That's in three days. We'll see."

"Deal," Peter said.

And they shook on it.

Peter had a few minutes to kill before sound check and there was only one thing he felt like doing to kill the time. And it wasn't his tutor's geometry homework assignment on vectors.

27

P—hey hey hey

    J—yay. Ur back!

P—ever play the ask-me-anything game?

    J—duh

P—K . . . you first. Only yes or no answers.

    J—no, you first

P—damn ur a tough one

    J—no, just dont like to make the first move hehe

P—ever?

    J—if poss. haha

P—hard being a guy, always gotta make the move
haha

    J—and ur question???

P—ok ok ok

P—thinking . . .

P—ever been to Tennessee?

    J—NO sadly. I want to though!!!

    J—do I still get to be ur friend?

P—is that an official question?

J—sure. haha

P—of course u do. YES --> Nobody from LA ever has been to Tenn. Youd be like the only 1 ever

P—ok, next quesht . . . hmmm

P—whats your favorite book?

J—so many I cant just say one. . .

J—Beowulf.

P—REALLY?

J—jkjkjkjkjkjk. That book is sooo boring! Had to write a book report on it and almost wanted to kill myself.

P—LOL

J—but honestly I really like The Great Gatsby.

P—wow, I just read that for school!

J—um you dont go to school. . . .

P—well, my homeschool hahaha . . . my tutor is amazing. Why do you like Gatsby so much?

J—because the romances are so intense. Like they all have money, but they are obsessed with what they dont have—LOVE. People always want most the thing they dont have. Kinda profound. . . . And plus I like reading about rich people, since I am so not rich. At all FYI!

P—rich is overrated, trust me. And, sorry but I didnt like the book so much. Maybe because it hits close to home . . . and it was kind of depressing!

J—why?

P—well, because basically everyone dies. And it is so cynical about wealthy people

J—r u ever cynical?

P—only when I realize I am not living the life I want to live, or when I feel like I am doing something for the wrong reasons.

J—like . . .

P—like not being friends with a girl just because im afraid of what people will say or cuz I dont trust someone. But I trust you. . . .

J—;)

P—ok, I have one more question before I gotta go to work

J—go for it

P—do u believe in God?

J—yes.

P—why?

J—Because I believe in love. And God is love.

From: TheTruthMustBeTold@gmail.com

To: johnny.love@omc.com

more info!

In all the time I have been tipping off your website, I've never been wrong. I have never given you a tip that wasn't true. I guarantee you that the Peter Maxx Marriage story is true. He did propose to Sandy. But she said no because she felt they were too young, though she loves him crazily. Of course, he is denying it ever happened to save face. Why? Because there is an even bigger story about to come out about Peter's love life and he doesn't want to look bad. HE is obsessed with his image. The god's honest truth is that he has a secret GF. Not Sandy. In fact, poor Sandy doesn't even know about it herself. In fact, Sandy is totally in the dark and, well, you gotta really feel bad for the girl. She is blinded by her love, I suppose, as are many young girls in her position. Poor girl. All I can tell you is that you should have a photographer staking out the lobby of the Palazzo hotel in Vegas this Friday. I wish I could tell you more, but I have been sworn to secrecy.

Packing for a trip to Las Vegas is no easy task. Especially when you've never been there and your only scant knowledge is pretty much what you've gleaned from TV and movies and those funny commercials. Especially when your mom can't know you're packing for Vegas because, if she did, you would be grounded for life. Especially when your closet isn't exactly brimming with outfits that scream "Las Vegas." Luckily, Josie had one day before she and D slipped out of town and made the five-hour drive across the Mojave Desert into Nevada.

Even though Josie knew she would be spending less than forty-eight hours in Vegas, the trip suddenly seemed complex fashion-wise. First off, there would be a Peter Maxx concert, which, naturally, meant a concert-appropriate outfit. Josie figured kids in Vegas dressed a lot more glamorously than kids in Bakersfield, so she pulled out everything that sparkled, including a tank top with silver sequins and a black blouse with a swirly design made of silver beads. As for shoes, she tried on a pair of black platform sandals she hadn't worn since last year and black boots that zipped up to just below her knee. They both fit, but barely. She had grown two inches taller and a half shoe size bigger in the last six months.

The last time Josie had actually enjoyed wearing a skirt

was when she was four and wore her Snow White dress like every day. She didn't like skirts. They weren't very practical, and she thought they made her legs look too skinny. Nevertheless she noticed that Sandy Jones almost always wore them, which led Josie to conclude that she probably should. Peter must have liked them. She would have to suck it up and wear one—at least one of the nights.

She pulled from her drawer a black cotton skirt she'd gotten last Christmas from her grandmother. It had been knee-length, but when she tried it on, it only covered halfway down her thigh. Josie stretched it down, wiggled her hips and adjusted it as low as she could without looking like a total slob. She filled her suitcase with the "best" of everything she owned: her *best* pairs of shorts, her *best* TOMS, her *best* two tanks (a black and a white), her *best* pairs of jeans, her *best* two-piece black bikini, all of which she modeled in front of her bedroom mirror. "Thank you, Peter," she said to the invisible pop star standing beside her at an invisible hotel pool. "I will have a Diet Coke, my love." Thank God, there wasn't a hidden camera in her bedroom.

Josie, still in her bikini, grabbed a towel, stuffed the tiny, old-school Samsung cell she had borrowed from Christopher into her bikini top and stepped out of her room. "Mom, I'm going to lay out on the grass for a little bit," she announced through the wall to the kitchen where her mom was cleaning.

"How's packing going?"

"Good," Josie replied. "Hard to pack for camping since I

haven't camped in *ages*."

"Do you have bug spray?"

"Um, no, but Ashley said she'd have all the hard-core camping stuff. She said it would be like staying in a hotel." Josie walked out the front door before her mom asked too many more questions that might catch her in her giant lie of the century.

Josie unrolled her towel onto a patch of grass in front of her apartment building and lay down on her back under the midday sun. If she could afford it, she would spend twenty bucks at a tanning salon, but seeing as though she had given D all her money (except for twenty bucks for spending), she had to tan herself the old-fashioned way.

Josie massaged the muscles in her palms, rubbing especially hard in the area just below her thumbs. They were sore from texting. She and Peter had been texting a lot over the last couple days about just about everything. About her family (though she still hadn't told him the little fact about her dad being in jail for operating an illegal marijuana farm). About her life in Bakersfield, about her high school drama, about some of her favorite songs she'd written. He asked a lot of questions, a quality that Josie believed showed true intelligence. Late last night, after he had gotten back to his hotel in Denver, she had texted him a few lines from a song she had written about being a big sister.

> P—wow, these are awesome. Where did you learn
> to write?

J—whadya mean?

P—your lyrics . . . they r like poetry!

J—I guess im a poet and I dont even know it.

P—HAHAHAHAHA

J—☺

Peter shared that he and his dad had been arguing a lot—and that he often missed his mom.

P—sorry if im being a buzzkill

J—not at all. No one is more emo than me

P—nah, I bet I top you, 4 sure

J—we will see in vegas

P—you mean VEGA$$$$$!!!

J—oh right. Vega$$$$$$$ hahahaha

P—this might be hard to believe, but being on the road is sorta lonely to be honest

J—like how?

P—I feel so detached from reality. City to city. Hotel to hotel. Plane to plane. Yea yeah I know it is hard to feel sorry for me

J—sounds like fun to me!

P—it is. Usually. I dont wanna be a brat. But when youre not able to just be urself, it isnt as fun as it can be. So many ppl around me, but they dont know the real me.

J—I feel same way. Well, except not cuz im

famous. But cuz ppl think im strange.

P—they do?

J—yeah. Im a supes loner.

P—so am i.

J—so perf! We can be loners together!

P—so funny. Totally

J—you should write a song about it.

P—about bein a loner?

J—well, yeah . . . or whatever is bugging you. It helps me a lot. Cheaper than therapy and cheaper (and better for you) than drugs.

P—truee . . . hahah. actually, to be totally honest with ya, I wrote a song about you on the plane the other day.

J—WHAT? For real?

P—uh yeah. Hehehe

J—no way. Don't believe u. sorry :/

P—youll see.

J—sucha tease u r.

P—;-) . . . k. gotta go, bedtiiiime. Gnite

J—nighty

As Josie lay on her towel soaking up the rays, she scrolled through the chat history, rereading their conversations over and over. It was all she could think about. All she wanted to think about.

"Josie!"

Connor was yelling from the top of the stairs down to his sister.

"Dad's on the phone!"

Dad. Definitely not what she wanted to think about.

Yet she had felt like a superbitch going MIA when he had called from jail earlier in the week, so she got up and began walking toward the apartment.

"Hurry!" Connor called out. "He's only got a minute and they shut it off."

Connor handed Josie the home phone before she even made it to the top of the stairs.

"Hey, Dad," Josie said unenthusiastically.

"Hey, baby." Josie could hear clanging and hollering in the background, as if he was calling from the middle of Game 7 of the NBA finals in Madison Square Garden and angry fans were making a racket. "I just wanted to say I'm okay, and I will be getting out of here soon. My lawyer is working on it. So don't worry."

"Okay," she said in a numb monotone. "Whatever you say."

"Look, Josie," he said. "I'm sorry about everything. Everything. I wish I could change it but I can't. But, look, it's all been a big misunderstanding, and it will all work out. I can't get into it, but, trust me, it will all work out—"

Josie didn't, couldn't, speak.

"I'm sure that, uh, you know, once everything gets pieced

together, this will all blow over. I mean, we got some piano playing to do, eh?"

When Josie didn't immediately respond, her dad continued, "Everything will be back to normal, baby."

"Whatever you say, Dad," Josie said coldly. "I mean, if you say so, it must be true."

Josie's mom stepped beside Josie and began eavesdropping. "Be nice," she whispered into Josie's ear.

"So Mom tells me that you're going camping this weekend, eh?" he said.

"Yeah. Old-school camping trip."

"That's good. Make sure you've got bug spray—and sunscreen, baby."

A clicking sound crackled on the line.

"Time's running out here, Josie. I'll call you soon, next time I can. Okay? Love you."

"Okay."

The line went dead.

Josie handed the phone to her mom while looking away. She stepped back outside, tiptoeing down the stairs to finish her bronzing session.

"What did he say?" Josie's mom asked.

"Does it really matter? It's all lies anyway."

30

"Please tell me you brought protection, Brant," Delilah said.

Josie twisted her neck abruptly to the left and wiggled in her car seat to face D. "Protection? Like a bodyguard?"

Delilah laughed, still not taking her eyes off the desert highway in front of her. "You know: BC. Rule number one: Never hit Vegas without BC."

"Seriously, D, I have no idea *what* you are talking about."

"Birth control. You know: BC."

"Oh. My. God. Why would I bring that?"

"Girl, if I have to tell you that, then you obviously weren't paying attention in Health Ed."

Until that moment, "Operation Sin City" (as D had decided to call their adventure) was working to perfection. Josie had never felt so free. It had been two hours since she had hugged her mom and Connor good-bye and had sneakily slipped into Delilah's black Honda Accord that awaited her behind a Dumpster on the other side of their apartment complex. About an hour into the drive, as D had blasted Coldplay and she had tapped her foot to the beat, Josie had looked around at the dull-brown expanse of cactus-and-scrub and had thought to herself that this was the farthest she had ever been away from home—without a parent. Sure, she had made day trips with friends down to L.A. to go shopping and hang out at the Santa Monica pier, but someone's mom or dad had driven them there and babysat them the entire time.

She could get out of the car and walk across the desert and no one would know where she was, who she was, or where she was going. For the first time in her life, she had felt like rather than belonging to someone else, out here, away from everyone and everything she knew and that knew her, she could only belong to herself.

Adult. That was the word that had come to her mind. She had felt so adult.

Then, somewhere east of Mojave and west of Barstow, Delilah had reminded Josie that maybe she was not as grown-up as she had thought.

Protection. Josie certainly knew what that meant. Duh, she'd taken that class in sixth grade. She knew how babies were made and her mom had—awkwardly—given her "the lecture." But, she had thought, that was stuff that older kids had to worry about. At least, until this moment on a desolate high-desert stretch of Route 58 when it struck Josie that she might be getting herself into something she wasn't yet prepared for, that maybe she was all of a sudden one of those "older" kids.

Delilah was doing nothing to calm her traveling partner's fears. She turned down the radio and chuckled.

"Brant, Brant, Brant," Delilah repeated with sighs of exasperation. "You're asking *me* why *you* might need protection? I mean, do you think this guy, who by the way is *sixteen*, is asking you to come all the way to Vegas—I mean VEGAS of all places—is putting you up in a hotel and is sexting you nonstop for the last week because he just wants to hang out like a couple of grade-school kids? He's a celebrity, Brant. He's a hottie. He totally has sex with fans. That is just what they do. Remember that Justin Bieber story?"

Josie thought about it for a few seconds. "Well, to be honest . . ." The car was heading east at about sixty m.p.h., but suddenly Josie felt like they were speeding toward Vegas at three times the legal limit—too fast for her comfort. "I actually do think he just wants to get to know me better. Sex has never come up once. He's not like that."

Delilah tilted her head to the right and glared over at her car mate. Arching her thick dark eyebrows, they formed an are-you-kidding me line of wrinkles in her forehead. "Really, Brant? I seriously don't wanna pee on your parade. I mean, this trip is gonna be epic sexy. Epic sexy. But I'm just keepin' it real."

"Honestly. I know it sounds naïve, but he's a different kind of guy. He's the kind of guy—"

"Guy," D interrupted. "Stop right there. Exactly my point! He is *a guy*. All guys say anything just to get in your pants. If they think you're a Bible thumper, they'll say they're born-again and say grace before dinner. If you say you like sensitive guys, they'll fake-cry during a movie just to make you want to sleep with them. Guys are dogs. Panting, pathetic, horny dogs." D looked back over at Josie, whose face had turned white as rice. "Even pretty emo boys like Peter Maxx."

Josie uncrossed and crossed her legs and sat up straight. "You don't know him. He's not like that at all. You're wrong."

"That's what I thought about Derek Gibbs."

"Who's that?"

"The dirt bag I lost my virginity to when I was around your age."

Josie's eyes lit up. She assumed D had done it, but wasn't sure. She was officially her first friend who had. "You were my age?"

"Well, yeah, I was fourteen. A young fourteen."

"What happened?" Josie asked.

D cruised past a tractor-trailer. "We were good friends at first. Like best friends. I liked him, but then one night we kissed and I realized I more-than-liked him, and so, basically, we started dating. He was a senior and I was a freshman, so I thought I was pretty cool dating an older guy like that. I mean, for weeks he bought me flowers, texted me little poems, treated me like a queen. And, I'm not gonna lie, he was *very* hot. Not kidding. He made me want to do things I had never done, Josie. You know, sex stuff. But, Josie, I have never told anyone this, but I wasn't ready for it. And, well . . . it was a bad scene."

D's shoulders slumped and her face softened. In the three years they had been neighbors, Josie had never seen D remotely look sad.

"What happened, if you don't mind me asking?" Josie hoped that D wouldn't start crying because if she did, it would be like finding out Santa Claus isn't real.

"I was at a pool party, and I got drunk—like an idiot." D gripped the steering wheel tighter. "And, well, he pushed things too far and I was too out of it—drunk off my ass—to stop him. By the time I realized what was happening, it was too late. I cried for the next month. Every day for a month."

"Did you tell your parents? Did they call the police?"

"My parents?" D glared at Josie. "If you haven't noticed, I don't exactly have real parents. I haven't talked to my mom in four years, and my dad would have blamed me somehow. Whatever."

Josie gently placed her hand on D's right shoulder. "I'm sorry. That sounds horrible."

"I survived," D said. "Lesson learned."

D noticed her travel partner staring blankly out the window at the desert scrub blurring by.

"Hey, Brant."

Josie looked back at her.

"I'm not telling you not to do anything with Peter. In fact, if you think it is right, then go for whatever. I'm just saying that there's more to life than sex. I know that when you haven't had it, you can make it out to be a bigger deal than it is. My advice: just chill and see what happens."

Josie cracked a smile. "Deal."

D slowed the car down and pulled into a minimart. She parked and noticed Josie was staring forward as if she had just witnessed a murder.

"Hey, seriously, so we are clear. I don't want to bust your buzz, Brant. I just don't want you to assume that everyone is as innocent and sweet and kind as you are. That's a big reason why I wanted to come with you. I mean, that and, duh, I've always wanted to go to Vegas."

D grabbed her purse from the backseat. "Let's get lunch. You hungry?"

"No. I'm good."

That, of course, wasn't entirely true. "Good" was the feeling that she was just a few hours from hanging out with a guy every teenage girl in the world would die to meet. Good was feeling independent for the first time in her life. Good wasn't now being afraid she was about to be pressured by an older boy to do things she wasn't ready to do.

While D browsed the junk food aisle, Josie sat alone in the car and pulled her cell from the cup holder.

She texted Peter.

almost there. Just checking in with ya

D returned to the car and got back onto the highway. A half hour later they were cruising past Barstow, just two hours from Vegas. Still, Peter had yet to reply.

"You know, Brant, you're a good kid," D said out of nowhere as they rolled through the middle of nowhere. "I was just thinking that I never really told you that. You're different. Embrace it. I like that you aren't afraid to let your freak flag fly. All those creeps at Lawndale are like robots."

"Thanks," Josie said.

"I mean, I know you've had to deal with people talking crap about you, bullying you around, or whatever."

"Not so bad. It would be worse if I actually had to be friends with most of them anyway."

"Word to that," D agreed.

"So did I tell you about Ashley?"

"Only that she's having a rad birthday party right now that you are supposedly at." D giggled.

"Well, we aren't friends anymore. After I got home from the jail, I called her and she told me she couldn't talk to me and that her mom wouldn't let us be friends. How lame is that? Whatever happened to loyalty?"

"I warned you about cheerleaders," D said ruefully.

"I know, I know."

"Trust me, Brant. You're better than her anyway. That chick has, like, zero integrity. She's like the anti-J. K. Rowling."

"Who?"

"J. K. Rowling. That lady who wrote all the Harry Potter books. She's the bomb. I'm a total Potterhead. I love those books. You've read them, right?"

"No, sorry, I'm not into that witch stuff. It freaks me out. I saw the movies. My brother was obsessed."

"Smart kid, that brother of yours. Well, if you read them you will learn everything you need to know about how to handle high school. J. K. Rowling was bullied as a kid and lived her life in books and daydreams and fantasy. She was an outsider. That's why her heroes are all outcasts and misfits." D looked over at Josie. "Like you and me."

Josie never took D as the bookish type. She was shocked—but she liked listening to her. Josie imagined this is what it would be like if she had an older sister, or a mom who talked to her like a girlfriend and not a child.

"What I'm trying to say, Brant, is that, well, you and me? Girls like us? We're the heroes. Those stupid popular girls? They're the zeroes."

D clenched her right hand and extended her knuckle at Josie, who bumped it back. It was the first time D ever fist-bumped her. Josie felt honored. D smiled and told Josie, "So we're friends, okay?"

"Okay." Josie smiled back.

"Just do me a favor. Please don't ever call me your BFF. Even if I am technically."

"Deal."

Josie thought of Ashley. She was probably up at the camp ground right about now, and all her perky cheerleader friends were sitting around gossiping about, well, probably her! She felt relieved not to be part of that circle. D didn't judge. D, as she said, kept things real.

Still, Josie's brain was filled with questions. Things that she didn't ask Peter—not because she was afraid to. Rather, she hadn't even thought to ask. *Does he expect me to stay in his room with him? Does he think I'm going to sleep with him? What if I say no? Will he not like me? Why isn't he texting me back?*

She needed answers. *Pronto*. The last thing Josie wanted was to get there feeling so unsure about the situation. She texted him again.

> hey 16. It's Almost 15. I have a quesht for you.
> Helloooo????

No reply.

Fifteen minutes later she texted him a picture of her sticking her tongue out and making a goofy face that belied the fact that her face was hot and she was having a mild panic attack.

Still, no reply. If it were night and if they weren't amid the lifeless desert scrub, there would be crickets chirping in the silence. It was deafening.

Sick of worrying, she cranked up the volume and for the next half hour Josie sang along to more Coldplay, rapped to Kanye West, and belted out "Empire State of Mind" (D did Jay-Z and she sang the Alicia Keys part).

"You have an awesome voice!" D enthused. "You sound like you should be on the radio. Damn, you got serious pipes."

Suddenly feeling self-conscious, Josie didn't know what to say.

"You should totally be singing your own songs. I mean, do you really like just writing songs?"

"Actually, I do. I love writing songs."

"I'd love to see some of them. I've never met a songwriter." D added, "For what it's worth, a few minutes ago, when you were singing along to that Coldplay song, well, I thought your voice was pretty hot. You can sing, chiquita."

"Nah, I wish. Singing in the car with you and singing in front of a group of people are two different things. I have big-time stage fright. I'm literally paralyzed by fear."

Delilah took her foot off the gas and rolled to a stop on the side of the highway.

"What are you doing?" Josie asked. "Why are you stopping?"

D didn't answer as she turned off the car and stepped outside into the hot desert air. Josie craned her neck and strained to look back as D opened the trunk and rustled through the mess inside. A minute later, D returned to the car and dropped a book in Josie's lap. Josie picked up the paperback, *Harry Potter and the Deathly Hallows*, and began thumbing through it as D started the car and pulled back onto the highway.

"What do you want me to do with this?" Josie asked.

"Read it, silly. It's like the seventh in the series, and I promise I'll give you the first ones, but, really, any of the Harry Potter stuff is amazing. One thing all these books are about, especially this one, is confronting your fears and finding the inner strength to overcome them. The thought that you are an amazing singer but too afraid to sing in front of people is beyond tragic to me. Life is too short to let your fears control you, girl."

Josie began reading the thick novel's first page.

"If you want to learn how to have sex with a vampire, read *Twilight*," D added. "If you want to learn how to be a total bad ass, read Harry."

An hour later, Josie was a hundred and fifty pages into the book. As they crossed the Nevada state line, D's beat-up black Honda was now covered in so much dust it looked more gray than black.

It was just after five o'clock and she hadn't heard from Peter all day. But then her phone buzzed awake.

have fun camping, amigo.

Christopher. They hadn't had any contact with each other since four days ago when they got into that spat at her house over her being a brat. She'd been avoiding him ever since. Not because she was still annoyed with him for calling her out, but because she wanted to keep her secret trip to Vegas just that: secret. She also didn't want to lie—that is, any more than she already had to her mom and brother. She decided she'd deal with Christopher after Vegas.

A few minutes later, D noticed Josie nervously checking her phone every ten seconds, and every time grunting in frustration. #GirlProblems.

"I'm sure he's just busy," D assured Josie. "He told us where to go, right?"

"Yeah, he said just go to the VIP check-in at the hotel, and everything would be taken care of."

Billboards for casinos, strip clubs, restaurants, golf courses, and hotels lined the freeway, which was filling up with more and more cars as they got closer to the city. Josie could feel her heart beating in her chest—a result of the excitement, uncertainty, and danger. She hated and loved the sensation all at the same time. D guided the car around a bend in the road, and in the distance at the bottom of the arid valley there it was: the Vegas skyline. "Check it out," Josie said, pointing into the distance.

D squinted and stretched her neck forward while sliding her sunglasses down the bridge of her nose. "It looks fake," she observed. "Like it isn't even real."

Josie just hoped that her connection with Peter wasn't a mirage.

⏮ ⏹ ⏭

"Good evening, Ms. Brant. We've been expecting you. We have you down for two nights in our VIP luxury suite."

The perky front desk clerk lady pointed at a uniformed old man standing next to the counter. "The bellhop over there will take your bags. Enjoy your stay at the Palazzo."

The lady handed Josie two envelopes. One contained two plastic card keys for their thirtieth-floor suite and two complimentary tickets to the Palazzo's long-running musical play *Jersey Boys*.

"Awesome," Josie said when she eye-balled the tickets. "The Four Seasons have the best love songs."

"I thought you said Peter Maxx did," Delilah deadpanned.

"Okay, make that second best."

As D and Josie followed the bellhop across the cigarette smoke-filled main casino floor to the elevator bank, Josie ripped open the other envelope. Inside, she found two tickets to that night's Peter Maxx concert at the MGM Grand Arena and a single VIP wristband and slip of paper, on which was printed:

The wristband in this envelope is your pass to a PRESHOW MEET-AND-GREET. Please get in the MEET-AND-GREET line next to the will-call ticket booth no later than 6:30 P.M. At 6:45 P.M. your ticket will be scanned and you will be escorted to the MEET-AND-GREET area. There will be NO AUTOGRAPH SIGNINGS and NO PERSONAL PHOTOS. A professional photographer will shoot your photo and you will be able to retrieve the photo at PeterMaxx.com. Enjoy the concert!

Now in the rising elevator heading up to her floor, Josie glanced at the clock on her phone: 5:20 p.m. Realizing they had just a little over an hour to get to their room, get dressed, and make it over to the arena on time, Josie breathlessly asked the bellhop, "Sir, how do we get to the MGM Grand Arena?"

"I'd say a taxi is probably the best way," the old man said.

"And how long will it take to get there?" she asked.

"Realistically, fifteen minutes," he said, stepping off the elevator and into the carpeted hallway. "Everything in Vegas takes fifteen minutes. Including losing everything you own or winning a million dollars."

The man chuckled and after passing a few doors down the

hall he stopped and swiped the key in the door and opened it. "Here you are, ladies! Enjoy your stay."

Josie ran into the room, a two-tiered suite with a king-sized bed on the upper level that sat two steps above a lower living room area. The suite was about the size of her apartment back in Bakersfield. Something, though, that was not the same: the breathtaking view of the Strip was a little better than the strip mall she could see from her second-floor apartment bedroom back home.

D scoped out the marble-and-mirror encased bathroom. "Okay, Brant," she declared from the walk-in shower stall. "I take back everything I said about Peter. This room is so sweet! I'm a fan."

Josie zipped open her suitcase and placed her black skirt and metallic tank top and black boots onto the bed. D dangled one of the black boots and joked, "Sexayyyy!"

"Hey, it's Vegas," Josie said with a shrug of her shoulders.

"Josie, we ain't in Bakersfield no more!" D said as she fell back onto the giant bed.

Josie's phone buzzed in her pocket.

> P—sorrry. Just got ur texts. Im alive. You get the tix? C u at meet and greet.

> > J—YES YES YES! Getting ready now with my friend.

> P—cool. Your friend knows to be secret right?

> > J—YES.

P—K. off to sound check. Cant wait to see you. Finally.

P—nervous?

       J—a little bit 2 b honest

P—me too. But in a good way. Excited. FYI I have a surprise 4 u at the show

       J—what is it????

P—if I tell ya it wont be a surprise

31

For Peter, the first of his two Vegas shows would be his twenty-fourth of the tour. The sound check, truth be told, had become more of a ritual to be done for the pleasure of radio contest winners who sat in the near-empty arena to hear bits of a few songs than an actual rehearsal of the venue's sound systems. But Peter dutifully did it a couple of hours before every show—just like he had been loyally fulfilling all of his professional obligations since he was a kid.

But suddenly he realized he didn't resent the commitments. He had a new outlook on his life. He decided he would no longer fight with his father. He would no longer complain about the restrictions placed on him by the Retro Records honchos. He wouldn't worry about Sandy Jones and what she was thinking about his decision to break up with her midtour. Nope. Peter had other plans. He was headed in a new direction.

Maybe the breakthrough came in his last meditation session when he realized he was ready to love. Maybe it is true, as he once read, that if you just start loving your life, then life will love you back. Starting tonight. And no one—not his dad, not his fans, not his agents, not his bandmates, not even Big Jim—knew what he would be doing, except for him.

After sound check, Big Jim escorted Peter back to his dressing room behind the stage. As Peter entered the locker room turned into a temporary dressing area, Sandy was walking out.

"Oh, hey, Peter! I was just looking for you."

"Well, here I am!" Peter said, throwing his arms in the air. "In my dressing room? Didn't you hear me at sound check?"

Sandy, still in her preshow sweatpants and hoodie, looked anxiously around the arena hallway. Her eyes darted from one end to the other. "Uh, I didn't actually. It's been such a crazy day."

"You sure you aren't looking for someone else?" Peter asked.

"Of course not, silly," she said. "I just wanted to wish you good luck tonight."

"Sandy, you never wish me luck. Seriously, what's up? You sure you are okay?"

Sandy grabbed Peter by the sleeve of his button-down shirt and pulled him aside, out of earshot of Big Jim. "Peter, I've had it with the attitude. Can't I come say hi to you without you acting weird about it? Truth is, I want to talk to you about our duet. The label wants us to do a promotional tour next month before it drops. It could be like, you know, awkward. So I think we should talk about how we are gonna go about it all."

"Look, Sandy," Peter said flatly. "It's a bad time right now. We can talk about this later. I gotta get dressed and over to the meet-and-greet. Let's talk later."

Sandy's face softened. "Sure. Okay. No worries. You're

right. We should talk when it's not so crazy." She hugged him and walked down to the G Girls dressing room as Peter and Big Jim locked eyes and shared an unspoken moment that said something along the lines of "Wow, that girl is wack!"

Along with the onstage sound check, another preconcert ritual was the meet-and-greet. Around thirty lucky fans—from contest winners, to friends and family members, to fan club devotees—had the chance to shake hands and take a photo with Peter before every show.

Because he only had from 7:00 to 7:15 p.m. to do all this, the whole event had the look and feel of a cattle call, with fans lined up outside a room in the basement of the arena and shuffling in one group at a time, with Big Jim hustling everyone along as quickly as possible.

If it were up to Peter he would spend a few minutes with everyone and get to know each one of them. It was the only part of concert days where he got to spend any quality one-on-one time with fans and he felt some sort of karmic responsibility to let fans get close to him, to give back some of the love that he felt for them—even if at times it could be exhausting to do so. It's an ethic that he credited his father with instilling in him. For all of his father's slick money-making chicanery, Peter had to give the man credit for always minding what Bobby called "the fan experience."

This meet-and-greet, though, would be different than any of the others.

"Remember, people! Turn off your phones," Abby instructed

the fans in queue. "And only one photo. Peter will meet everyone, but we have to make each one very quick. The number you were given out front is your place in line. So everyone please get in order and we will start the meet-and-greet." The fans jostled for position.

Fifteen minutes later, Peter first heard her, the heels of her knee-high black boots clicking on the cement floor as she entered the room. Her tight-fitting black skirt came to just halfway down her thigh, and her metallic-silver tank stuck to her chest. A padded bra added a shape she didn't have the first time Peter met her.

Peter's eyes scanned her from foot to face, stopping on the dark eyes made even darker with eye shadow.

"Well, look at you!" Peter hugged her, even more tightly than the first time. "I barely recognized you!"

"I hope in a good way," Josie replied with a nervous smile.

"You kidding me?" Peter beamed. "In a great way!" He looked her up and down—again. "You just look . . . different."

"I don't usually dress like this. But, you know, it's Vegas and all so . . ." Josie self-consciously began tugging downward on her skirt. "Probably the eyes. My friend D says that smoky eyes add like five years to a face."

"No worries. You look amazing."

Peter took her hand and walked her to a spot in the room in front of a Peter Maxx photo backdrop, placed his arm affectionately around her, and smiled for the snapshot.

"Wait, one sec," he said after the flash. He pulled out his

phone and, extending his arm out as far as he could, he took a picture of them with his phone. "That one's for me," he whispered. "I don't have a pic of you for my phone."

He then professionally shook her hand, pressing into her palm a plastic card and said, "Room 5320. Meet you there after the show for our writing sesh. Shhh."

Josie smiled. "Enjoy the show," he said, leaning in and kissing her on her right cheek. "And, remember, there's a surprise."

32

Trying to explain what it feels like to have Peter Maxx kiss you gently on your cheek after handing you his hotel room key and a flirtatious note is like trying to explain what it feels like to be shot into space while strapped to a rocket. The head-to-toe tingling. The sense of weightlessness as you ascend up beyond the Earth's gravitational pull. The force, the thrust, the intense feeling of being catapulted into a limitless space brimming with unknown, exciting possibilities. That feeling, one that you will never forget after experiencing it, embeds every cell of your body as you make your way onto the arena floor and take your front-row seat next to your new confidante, a girl who is older and wiser and something of a savior.

And the sensation continues as you sit through the opening set of the G Girls and you watch one of the girls, the blonde, Peter's ex, dancing and singing and you keep thinking how she's so beautiful and you realize that her flawless face shares something in common with yours, that it has been kissed by that gorgeous Rocket Boy.

The feeling continues throughout the night as you stand and sing along to every song he sings because you've memorized all the lyrics and because you always felt they spoke to you—and now, as he gazes down at you and smiles several times each song, you realize that they really are. You realize that you're in deep, that no matter how nervous you might be about this new relationship, that there is some nature of inevitability and fate *that is beyond your control. You've never felt like this before, the lightness of being that has you feeling like your feet are levitating just above the floor. You would call it an out-of-body experience, but the experience is entirely within your body, deep into its core, and you realize that, no matter what happens from this moment forward, life will never be the same.*

He ends the first set with one of your faves, "No Regrets," and after several minutes of chanting from the fans, he comes back out for the encore. He sits down on a stool with nothing but his acoustic guitar, looks down at you, and while gently strumming the guitar, starts talking to the packed arena: "I have a little surprise."

Your stomach tenses when you realize he is talking to you.

"Everyone needs a muse. Out on the road, I've been doing some reading. And I've learned that every artist, poet, great thinker throughout history has had a muse. And for me it is you, the fans. But this next song is about a special muse I met recently, and she's here tonight. This is a new song I've written. It's called 'So Down with You.'"

The stage lights go down and, under a single spotlight, he sits strumming the prettiest sounding chords you've ever heard in your life and you can't take your eyes off his lips as he sings a song delivered like poetry of a melodious kind you've never heard before. . . .

> *Down below my jet window I see*
> *Beating hearts of humanity*
> *A pickup rolls down a dirt road*
> *And I wonder who's inside*
> *A boy like me? Where's he going?*
> *No way of knowing*
> *But I wish that was me and I was . . .*

So down with you
Taking the road that leads me to you
So down with you
Flying so high but wishing I could be
Down in love with you

From my plane's sight, I wonder if he's lonely,
     if he's all right
Does he have a good life?
Maybe a wife?
Has he known a loved one's death?
Does he treasure his every breath?

His truck rolls away in the opposite direction
I wonder if he's known true love connection
Like the kind I feel when I am . . .

So down with you.
I hope he's had my kind of luck
A man like me who's so, so, so
So down with you . . .
'Cuz baby I'm so down with you. . . .

33

Josie Brant's heart had melted, and the puddle ran its way back to the Palazzo's tower, to the very top floor, to the Prestige Siena Suite—Room 5320—where she sat alone on the most comfortable couch she had ever sat in waiting for Peter to return.

It had been a long day. She hadn't had a good night's sleep in over a week. Every bone in her body ached with exhaustion. Eleven became eleven thirty and then it became almost midnight, and as much as she didn't want to, she lay her head on the coziest pillow she'd ever placed her head on and drifted off to sleep. And when she came to some time later she was looking in the dark eyes of Peter.

"So, did my singing put you to sleep?" he asked her gently.

"Hardly." She rubbed her eyes and let out a cough, self-conscious of her breath. She put her hand up to cover her mouth and made a gross face.

Peter laughed and assured her, "No morning breath. It's only midnight."

"Did you like the song?"

"Of course, I did."

Peter handed her a glass of water. "Here, drink up. Vegas tends to dry people out."

Josie sipped from the glass, squishing the water around her mouth before swallowing it in a gulp.

"Are you sure it's cool for me to be in here with you?" she asked. "I don't want you to get in trouble."

This was Josie's out. Anxious about what might happen if she did stay in that room all alone with him, a part of her (a very small, scaredy-cat part) was hoping he'd say, "Yeah, it's probably not a good idea. You should go back to Bakersfield." But he didn't.

"It's all good. Everyone's asleep." Peter stood up and sat on the chair next to the couch. "Everyone, obviously, except for us."

Josie realized this was the first time she was ever alone with Peter. It felt surreal yet entirely normal at the same time. There was an energy of familiarity between the two that put her at ease, that made it seem like they'd known each other forever. An energy that made her feel like she could ask him anything. And, unlike her dad, she would trust she'd get an honest answer.

"So is that song really about me?"

Peter nodded. "Sorry I didn't call out your name. Not sure the world is ready to hear that I have a crush on someone, especially since they still think I'm dating Sandy."

A crush? #OMFG.

Josie flashed her best poker face, hoping she showed no evidence of her shock.

"But how can you write a song about me when we had only met once?"

"Because you're my muse."

"You realize you're crazy, right?"

Josie sat up straight on the couch. Definitely not groggy anymore, she crossed her arms in front of her chest. This was all happening so fast. She had to say something.

"My friend D thinks you just want to sleep with me," she blurted. "She says guys will say anything just to get what they want."

"Who's D?" Peter laughed.

"My neighbor. She drove us here. She's down in my room."

"Well," Peter said, getting up and grabbing a guitar from the case on his bed, "D sounds like a smart girl because most guys do. Not gonna argue that one."

Peter sat down on the couch next to Josie. Nestling the guitar in his lap, he added, "But if it makes you feel any better, I am probably more nervous than you are right now."

"I seriously doubt that."

"Why do you think I picked up this guitar? It's like my security blanket. Honestly, I have no idea what I'm doing. I'm just flying on autopilot here. I mean, A, my dad would kill me if he knew you were here. And B, my fans would freak out. And C, you could be a total Stan."

"A 'Stan'?"

"You know, like a stalker fan."

"Obviously, I'm a fan," she said playfully. "But I'm no stalker."

"How do I know that?" Peter smiled wryly.

"For starters, you are the one who invited *me* here."

"You got me there. Okay, okay, okay. I admit it. I stalked you. Guilty. I guess inviting someone to Vegas who you've only met once is kind of creepy." Peter laughed and set the guitar in his lap and picked a couple chords gently. Josie turned to face Peter and watch him play, leaning back on the armrest and sitting cross-legged while pressing her hands self-consciously into her skirt so it covered her thighs.

Josie watched his left fingers contort up and down the frets, noticing how they glided across the strings with strength and gentleness at the same time. Playing the guitar was an enviable talent. Playing the guitar with poetic grace and sexiness was downright godly.

As much as Josie wished she could be the cool girl, the lucky fan sitting alone in Peter Maxx's hotel room, and just go with the flow and do whatever came naturally, Josie didn't. She felt like an eager skydiver who had trained a year to jump from a plane, and just when she was to take the leap into the air, freezing in fear. Maybe some things were best left to fantasy. Maybe, she thought to herself, her dad was right: you don't want to meet your heroes. Maybe they were something best left at a distance. Maybe texting and Tweeting and sitting in the front row at a concert was close enough, maybe that was the healthy distance between a fan and a pop star.

Josie watched Peter's fingers hypnotically glide up and down the neck of the guitar—strong and gentle at the same time. The spacious hotel suite seemed smaller and smaller, getting darker and darker.

A panic attack: Panting. Sweating. Chest rash.

Peter immediately put down his guitar.

"Are you okay?"

Josie shook her head "no" and her eyes fluttered.

Peter placed his right hand behind her head and gently cupped his left hand under her knees, placing her on her back on the couch.

"Josie, just breathe. You're not breathing."

Peter knelt beside the couch and sucked in a deep inhale. "Breathe with me, Josie. Through your nose, fill your lungs, and then"—he exhaled—"out through your nose."

When her dad had gotten arrested in front of her, and when she had watched as her former BFF betrayed her, and whenever else she had ever suffered a panic attack, she had stopped breathing. Usually, she would just ride it out and wait for her body to calm itself. Not this time.

Peter placed his hand on the middle of her chest. "Keep your eyes closed and keep breathing with me," he instructed her softly. "In and out. Feel the oxygen coursing through your body, feel it relaxing you."

Eight or nine breathes later, Josie's breathing slowed back to normal.

"What just happened?" Josie said a few minutes later, peeling open her eyes.

Peter smiled. "Just keep your eyes closed and breathe. You

meditated. You calmed yourself."

Josie rubbed her eyes. "Wow."

"Josie, I used to take Ambien to help me sleep because I would be so nervous, so wound up, so neurotic about things that I couldn't just chill and fall asleep. Then I learned how to breathe."

Josie nodded. She felt so comfortable in his care. Her body sunk into the couch.

"I feel so stupid," she said, the room finally coming into clear focus. "I don't know what's wrong with me."

"The reason you don't know is because nothing is wrong with you. You're just human. It's okay."

Peter looked at her brightly. "You're fine now, right? Better?"

"Amazing."

Josie rubbed her eyes and sat up slowly, staring blankly around the room, squinting them more into focus. Staring straight into Peter's dark eyes, Josie noticed that his were already locked on hers.

Peter reached in with his right hand and took the hair strands falling down the side of her cheek and with two fingers delicately tucked them back behind her earlobe.

Josie's lips curled upward into a smile. Peter tilted his head to the side, his eyes fixing on her lips. Their bodies were speaking a language to each other that needed no interpretation, no explanation, no words.

Still kneeling beside the couch, Peter tucked a few more

strands of her hair behind her other ear, and with neither taking their eyes off the other until their mouths met and their eyes closed, they—finally—kissed.

34

KNOCK-KNOCK-KNOCK.

The jarring thuds on the hotel room door came in a rapid-fire of threes.

KNOCK-KNOCK-KNOCK.

Peter leapt to his feet.

KNOCK-KNOCK-KNOCK.

Peter placed his forefinger in front of his lips and hushed "shhh" to Josie who lay still on the couch.

"PETER, OPEN IT UP. WE NEED TO TALK!"

"*Dad,*" Peter mouthed to Josie, grabbing her by the hand and lifting her to her feet. Josie picked up her phone from the coffee table as Peter guided her to the front of the suite and into the bathroom. The toilet area had a room and door of its own.

"Hide in here," Peter told her, closing the door quietly then walking out, closing the main bathroom door behind him. "Coming, Dad. Hold on!"

"What *the hell* were you doing out there tonight?" asked Bobby, hands on hips.

Peter turned his back and walked back to the couch, kicking Josie's black boots underneath so his dad wouldn't notice. Luckily, he didn't.

"You just can't play a song that's never been rehearsed. We talked about this, remember?"

Bobby paced back and forth and nervously combed his fingers through his hair. "And that banter about your muse. A muse? Really? Muuuuuse? I mean, who the heck is, all of a sudden like, your muuuuuse? Poor Sandy."

Bobby kept pacing. Peter just sat on the foot of the bed watching him dart around.

"At first, I had assumed the song was about her, and then I see her bawling backstage afterward. So I am sure as hell it ain't her, Peter."

Peter looked away.

"Son," he fumed. "You've been acting nuttier than a freakin' squirrel turd lately. We need to figure this out, because this"—Bobby motioned his hands in and out between him and his son—"is just not working anymore. I think that is one thing me and you can agree on."

"I totally, one-thousand percent agree," Peter said. "This is not working at all. That is exactly what I have been trying to tell you for the last couple weeks. I am a teenager; I am not perfect, and I am tired of pretending to be perfect. It's not working because I'm getting a mind of my own and you can't handle it. I wrote one song. I sang it. One song! And you freak out about it. I can't just live *your* dreams anymore, Dad. I have to live mine."

Peter rarely raised his voice to his dad. Not because he was afraid of him. Though Peter could get frustrated with him, at the end of the day he respected him. But this time it felt necessary. He didn't feel shame or guilt. He felt empowered.

Bobby kept shaking his head. "Son, if it weren't one in the freakin' morning I would sit down with you and hammer this out. I don't want to fight with you. I want you to be happy. It's just we have commitments, and sometimes in life we may not feel like fulfilling them, but we committed so we do them. Am I makin' sense?"

"Yes, Dad, you're making sense. I'm not gonna stop doing anything. That means I'm not gonna stop touring and working hard for you, me, and everything we've built. But I'm also not gonna stop being me. I'm just doing some things I need to do for myself. I need to have a life that isn't being a pop star. I just want to be real. I want to feel *normal* for a change."

Bobby's cheeks sunk in and his shoulders slumped like the air had been let out of him. He shuffled over to Peter, and lowered his voice. "But you ain't normal, Peter. That horse left the barn a loooong time ago."

Peter didn't know what to say. His dad was right.

"But I get it," Bobby continued. "I'm a slow learner, but I get it. We can talk more later. We've got another show tomorrow, don't forget."

Bobby hugged Peter and turned for the door. Luckily, for everyone in that room, hidden and otherwise, Bobby didn't randomly decide to go pee. Instead, he left the room for the night.

"Okay, shady lady," Peter announced from the main suite. "It's safe to come out now."

Josie slinked out of the bathroom and into the bedroom. "I had no idea. . . . I had no idea."

"How would you?" Peter plopped down onto the bed. "It's not something I've really told anyone—until now. I was hoping you heard that. Did you?"

"Yeah, kind of impossible not to. You really want to be a *normal* kid? I mean, it's not as glamorous as you might think. There's homework, stupid classmates, boredom, no money to buy things, all that kind of stuff."

Peter picked back up his guitar and began quietly fingerpicking while he listened to her.

"I can see how you are feeling like you have to be 'on' all the time. That would suck, definitely."

Peter stared out the window at the bright flashing lights.

"But, also, maybe you just should appreciate what you have," she continued. "You do have a pretty cool life."

"That's what my dad says." Peter grumbled.

Josie paused.

Peter broke the silence.

"What do you think I should do?"

Josie shifted her weight to her left foot and then to her right.

"Well, I can tell you what I do when I'm upset," she offered.

"What's that?"

"I write songs." She shrugged her shoulders. "I just write songs."

"I used to do that."

"But you still write. I heard that song tonight. It was amazing. That song was so real. That was the most real thing I've heard out of anyone's mouth in a long time. You are a real person, Peter."

"Not as real as you. That's why I like you so much. That why I wanted you to come see me."

"So you just didn't want me to come so you could cure my panic attacks and kiss me?"

Peter laughed. "Josie, the truth is, I'm an okay singer, a pretty capable guitar player, but I can't write songs for crap."

"You're messing with me, right?" Josie snapped back. "Your songs move people. They're so real."

"Yeah, pretty ironic isn't it?"

"No, not at all. It would make sense that your songs would connect with real people, real emotions, because you're feeling like it is hard for you to most of the time. Music is your outlet. It's the same for me."

"Well." Peter sighed. "I knew I asked you here for a reason."

"For what reason exactly?"

"To do this." Peter motioned back and forth with both his hands. "You know: Talk. Just be us. Have this kind of connection we have. I want this. Not another hit song. Not another million fans." Peter stepped closer to Josie. She braced for another kiss. "I know this is kinda cheesy sounding," he said tentatively. "But you get me."

Josie looked down at his feet.

"I'm serious," Peter said, lifting her chin up with his hand. "And you're a good kisser."

Josie twirled her hair.

"Don't be so hard on yourself about the songwriting. If it makes you feel any better, I can't *sing* for crap."

"Oh, really?" he asked with a grin. "Let me hear. I will be the judge of that. Show me."

"No way."

"Please," he begged. "Just sing anything."

She locked her lips with an imaginary key and pretended to throw it over her shoulder onto the bed.

"I bet you don't wanna sing because you don't want me to hear just how good you are."

"I wish."

"Fine." Peter grabbed his guitar case from the floor by the couch and flipped it open. "I have an idea. How about I sing 'Down with You.' And you can sing along. We'll make it a duet. That way it's not just you out there naked."

Josie puckered her lips and scratched her chin, as if in deep thought, and Peter suddenly began strumming the opening chords of the song.

"Wait, I didn't agree!" she exclaimed. "I don't even know all the words."

"I took that cute expression you make with your lips as you agreeing," he said with a smile and began singing. "As for the words, just follow my lead."

Down below my jet window I see
Beating hearts of humanity. . . .

Taking a higher octave, Josie joined. Peter nodded and kept strumming and singing in perfect harmony and staring into her eyes, then he looked down at the red smudge of lipstick on the lips that a few minutes ago he had just kissed for the first time.

The two smiled at each other as they sang and stared into each other's eyes.

"You know," Josie said. "This is the part of the story where you are supposed to kiss me again."

"Yeah, I know. I've seen the movies."

Josie licked her lips.

"Would you like a glass of water?" he asked.

"Why?"

"Because your mouth looks like the Sahara."

"That's what happens when someone's nervous, duh."

"You know, there's a cure for that," Peter said, stepping closer. Being a good five inches taller than her, he tucked his chin.

"Oh, really?" Josie asked. "Does it involve breathing in and out?"

Peter answered by closing his eyes and pressing his lips against hers.

And by the time the kissing ended minutes later, they lay next to each other on the bed side by side, for the first time as comfortable physically as they had always been mentally.

35

"**Have you ever** been in love, Josie?" Peter asked out of nowhere.

"I don't think so," she answered. "What about you?"

Peter rolled from his side onto his back and stared up at the chandelier dangling above the comfy king-size bed.

"I thought I was with Sandy, but then I realized I wasn't," he confessed.

"Why'd you break up?"

"We got into an argument—after the Bakersfield show as a matter of fact—and in the middle of the fight all I could do was look at her and think, 'This girl is attractive, talented, and says she loves me, but I just don't belong with her.' It was like an epiphany." Peter still stared up toward the ceiling and continued, "Then, the next day, I met you. Funny how life works out."

"So then your answer is 'no'? You've never been in love."

"So far, no, I've never been *in love*. But, I can't lie. I'm definitely *in something* with you."

Josie didn't know how to reply. Every bone in her body vibrated with the feeling of being in love. Or was it just lust? Obsession? Maybe she was merely starstruck? She didn't know.

"How do you even know when you're 'in love'?" he asked.

"I mean, what's the feeling?"

Josie sat up. "I think it's when you feel like a missing puzzle piece finally has been found."

Peter smiled. "And is that it?"

"No," Josie added. "I imagine that you also know you're in love when there is no doubt, no questioning. When you can't see a future without the person. When you get that nervous feeling inside your stomach every time you walk into a room and see them. When you feel like you would die without them. When that person is the first person you think about when you wake up and the last person you think about before going to bed. When you want to share everything that happens to you and everything you are thinking with that person. It's the feeling that you can truly be your real, true self around them, and them with you."

"Wow, you've definitely given this a lot of thought," Peter said before Josie could take another breath to keep her speech going. Which she did.

"When my mom was going through the divorce, one of her friends gave her a card," Josie breathlessly continued. "And it had the best quote ever in it: 'Love is the most beautiful of dreams and the worst of nightmares.' I just love that—"

"Shakespeare," Peter interrupted.

"Huh?"

"That's a quote from Shakespeare."

"Really? Wow, I just liked it. Look at you, Mr. I-don't-go-to-school!"

Josie watched Peter flash his perfect white teeth, revealing a cute set of dimples on each cheek to match, her awe bringing her to an abrupt halt.

"Just because I don't go to school doesn't mean I don't read," he said proudly. She just stared at him.

"Go ahead, continue," Peter encouraged her.

Josie couldn't. She wanted to tell him the truth why she couldn't talk: his beauty had literally taken her breath away. A voice inside her wanted to tell him that this was another sign of true love. But she didn't. Not yet. She didn't want to freak him out.

She walked over to the hotel room's bedside table, twisted open a bottle of water, and took a swig. Peter watched adoringly from across the room. "Seriously, Josie. Keep talking. I love it."

Josie blinked hard and refocused. She felt human again.

"Well, something I have been obsessed with lately is the whole idea of how there's a difference between being able to quote-unquote 'love' someone and being 'in love' with them."

"Tell me the difference," he said.

"Well, my friend Ashley—the girl you met—she's always saying that I'm in love with my best guy friend, Christopher," Josie explained. "But I'm definitely not. I mean, I love my Christopher, but I am not 'in love' with him. I can't really say why, it's just the feeling is different. It's not the kind of feeling like I have for—"

Josie's pause made it obvious what she was about to say;

Peter's smile spoke for him.

"And you know what, Peter Maxx?" she continued.

"What's that, Josie Brant?"

"You definitely know you're in love when . . ."

"When what?"

Josie looked down. Quickly glancing back up, she looked into Peter's eyes and said, "You know you're in love when every love song on the radio makes you think of that person."

From: (TheTruthMustBeTold@gmail.com)

To: (johnny.love@omc.com)

homewrecker!

I take it you got the pictures of the Bakersfield girl in Vegas. I know they don't prove anything because she isn't with Peter in those pics. But this photo I have attached of the two of them should be all the PROOF you need. Also, I have attached a series of texts they have been sharing. Total truth.

Mr. Love, I have never lied to you. I have given you so many stories over the last year. All true.

So, remember, THE TRUTH MUST BE TOLD.

Best wishes,

Your secret source

P.S. They're still in Vegas.

In the fog of morning, it was hard for Josie to know for certain whether her life as she remembered it before she fell asleep was real.

She was not sure if she really did kiss a boy she never in a million years thought she would ever meet, let alone make out with all night long. Not sure if the sweatpants and T-shirt she was wearing were his as she rubbed her eyes awake. Not certain about anything because everything felt so different, so magical.

But then came a wake-up call. First, in the form of a shout of disbelief—"Are you kidding me?"—from the boy as he stared at a laptop on the desk across from her bed.

And, secondly, in the form of that boy stomping over to the bed in a huff and angrily dropping the computer onto her lap and saying, "I can't believe you did this to me!"

She read the OMC story with a picture of her and Peter lovingly staring into the camera.

Peter Maxx Cheating Scandal: Sex, Drugs, and Vegas!

So much for Peter Perfect. OMC has exclusively uncovered the shocking news that pop superstar Peter Maxx, 16, has been secretly having a romance with a 14-year-old California fangirl. As you can see in our exclusive photo of the two sharing an intimate moment just yesterday in Vegas, the secret couple has taken their affair to Sin City, right under the nose of Peter's longtime girlfriend, G Girls singer Sandy Jones.

"Poor Sandy," says a Maxx insider. "She was so in love with Peter. But then he goes and does this. If there is any silver lining, Sandy will have a good heartbreak song to sing about this. But mostly she is just devastated."

Sources tell OMC that the mystery brunette is named Josie Brant, a fan Peter met recently during a promotional appearance at a Bakersfield high school. Peter kept the relationship secret, especially from his girlfriend, until now.

OMC has obtained intimate text messages that Peter and his secret lover shared. Among them, this revealing exchange:

P—truee . . . hahah. actually, to be totally honest with ya, I wrote a song about you on the plane the other day.

J—WHAT? For real?

P—uh yeah. Hehehe

As for the homewrecking hottie, OMC has uncovered shocking details about the girl that threaten to stain the pop star's squeaky-clean, all-American image.

OMC has learned that Josie Brant and her father, a former pro hockey player, were detained and arrested by police just last weekend during a raid of her father's Bakersfield-area farm. Police reportedly found 1,160 marijuana plants on the property with a street value of $4.6 million, along with another 55 pounds of cultivated pot worth about $220,000. Josie's father remains in custody on $5 million bail and is awaiting trial. If convicted, he faces up to ten years in state prison. As for Josie, charges may be pending. Police declined to comment, however, citing the ongoing investigation.

Little else is known of Josie Brant, who has a Twitter name of "MusicLuvr" and has just 78 Facebook friends, yet sources tell OMC that she aspires to be a famous songwriter and many of her high school classmates believe she is using Peter for that reason.

Meanwhile, sources tell OMC that, as of the time this story was posted, the new couple was holed up at the Palazzo Las Vegas Resort Hotel.

Josie's mouth gaped open as she read the story and she couldn't suck in air.

"How could you do this to me?" Peter shouted. "What are you, some kind of psycho monster?"

Josie couldn't unfreeze the muscles in her face or chest or anywhere in her body to take in enough oxygen into her lungs. She looked at Peter with glassy eyes, and the room began spinning. She tried to breathe. But the air wouldn't go in.

Peter locked his hands behind his head and looked up at the ceiling. "So you hacked my phone and sent those OMC losers the picture of us I took last night at the meet-and-greet? And then you sent them all of our texts? And I trusted you!" Peter pointed his finger at her, and his voice shook unevenly. "You, of all people. I thought you were different. I trusted you."

Peter barked at Josie, but not in the spit-spewing way her dad used to yell at her mom in the last days of their marriage when he would come home drunk and they would argue. The trauma of those fights, when Josie would bury her head under her pillow trying not to hear, came back to her in this moment.

Short breath. Tight chest. Sweating palms. Rash on her cheeks. Josie's PTSD symptoms kicked in full-force. Only this time, Peter didn't offer to cure them with his meditative breathing techniques.

"I should have listened to my dad," he said, kicking his guitar to the floor. The strings vibrated in the silence. "You burned me good, Josie."

Josie finally found strength to speak up, albeit shakily. "I swear it's not what it looks like. I didn't leak anything. I didn't hack you. I have no idea how this stuff got out. I swear to God, Peter. I swear. To. God."

"Yeah, right," Peter said angrily.

Choking back tears, Josie stomped toward Peter and slapped her cell phone into his hand. "Look for yourself. Go through my phone. I swear, I didn't send anything to anybody."

Peter quickly browsed through her sent folder. "Whatever." He dropped her phone onto the floor. "All this proves to me is that you know how to press delete. You could have sent them and erased it."

Just then, Peter's phone rang. "Hey, Big Jim," Peter answered. "No, it's okay. But, yeah, come up and get her."

Peter hung up and faced Josie. "And your dad's in jail? You'd think that might be something you would tell someone you cared about. Don't you realize how bad this makes me look? Everything I've worked so hard for could be ruined! By you."

"Well, yes, the jail part is true," she admitted, quickly adding, "but I wasn't the one arrested. It's a long story, but I have never touched a drug in my life, I swear to you. It was all a big mistake by my dad. I was just in the wrong place at the wrong time."

"So the jail part is true, but you expect me not to believe the rest of it? I can't believe this is happening. I believe nothing you're saying."

A stream of tears ran from her eyes and over her cheekbones, dripping down her face and chin. As she wiped them, she made a smudge of raccoon-like circles from her mascara.

"You have to believe me, Peter. Please believe me. I didn't tell anyone. I swear to you!"

He snapped, "That's not true. You told your girlfriend, remember?"

"Um, yeah, but I told you about that. I wasn't hiding anything. I'm telling the honest truth."

"Well, hotel security just escorted your friend off the property. I wish I could trust you, Josie. And, believe me, I want to believe you. I would want to do nothing more than be able to tell my dad that is was all just a big misunderstanding, that you did nothing wrong, and be with you like everything is just normal. I was falling for you, Josie. Falling hard. But now I can't. Just can't. And it breaks my heart. You broke my heart."

Peter's voice tailed off and, after a breath, perked back up. "As I see it, there are two people who could have sent those texts and that pic, and they are both in this room. And I can tell you this: it wasn't me. That leaves one person. I'm not stupid, Josie."

Peter bent over and gathered the skirt and tank on top of Josie's black boots. "I think you should put on your own clothes and leave," he said, handing them to her in a heap. "I'm sorry. But you have to leave. Now."

KNOCK-KNOCK-KNOCK.

Josie ran into the bathroom, and as she slipped out of Peter's clothes and into her own, she heard the door open and a voice say, "Where is she? Where is that girl?"

"Miss Brant," the voice shouted through the door. "I want you out of this room ASAP."

Josie slunk out in her black miniskirt, boots, and silver top and handed Peter his clothes. She couldn't catch her breath and, no matter how hard she tried, couldn't blink back the tears.

"If any media, or any paparazzi, asks you anything about this, you need to just shut up and walk," Abby instructed. "Got that?"

Josie wiped the sniffles from her nose with her forearm.

"Hey, easy on her, Abby," Peter said. "She's only fourteen."

"Easy on her?" Abby asked. "She hacked you, used you, and could damn well take us all down! So, no, I am not going easy on you, honey. Let's go."

Big Jim waited in the hall for Josie and when she walked out he pointed down the hall at the elevator bank, and she shuffled lifelessly along the carpet like a death row inmate on her way to her execution.

38

The paparazzi madness outside the hotel happened in a blur. The flashes. The questions: "WHY ARE YOU LEAVING? . . . DIDN'T YOU KNOW HE HAD A GIRLFRIEND? . . . WHERE'S PETER?"

She didn't know how she even made it to the SUV without falling down, fainting, or both. And, now, her forehead was bleeding like a UFC fighter. She assumed it was from being knocked by a photographer's camera, but she wasn't sure. There were so many things she wasn't sure about anymore.

Sitting in the backseat of Big Jim's SUV, she checked her phone and saw ten texts from Delilah, who had, in fact, been escorted out of the hotel in the morning as Josie slept. D's last text announced that she was already halfway back home to Bakersfield.

> They said they were flying you back and some fat old chick told me I should leave town or she'd have me arrested! Drama! C u back in Btown. Text me when u land. Sorry, Josie. This sux.

As the SUV approached the Vegas airport, where a private jet awaited her to whisk her back to Bakersfield, Josie dabbed the blood on her forehead with a tissue Big Jim had given her.

"I did nothing wrong," Josie told Big Jim. "I swear to you, sir, I didn't tell anyone, didn't leak a single thing to anybody. I don't know why this is happening. It's just so confusing. Why wouldn't Peter believe me?"

Big Jim steered into the aviation terminal parking lot and got out, opening Josie's door. Avoiding eye contact through his Ray-Bans, he pointed across the tarmac at a white Lear jet with the stairs folded down. "There's your ride. Have a good flight," Jim said, the hiss of the jet engines making it hard to hear.

Josie looked at the burly bodyguard and asked over the roaring engines, "Do you believe me?"

Big Jim placed his giant right hand on her shoulder and said, "Don't worry. I do believe you. Now just go home."

Josie slouched away and stepped onto the jet. She sunk into her window seat and pulled her phone from her backpack. Scrolling through the contacts to the P's, she stopped with a light tap of her forefinger and pressed on "Peter." She looked at his name and his 310-area code number. The more she stared at his name, the more she realized what she needed to do. This love song would not have a happy ending.

Delete.

39

"**Trust me.** This is all for the best," Abby said, pacing Peter's hotel suite like a caged tiger. "You don't need any more of this *drama* in your life."

Peter's publicist stepped in front to the room's giant swinging French doors. She twisted her neck side to side slowly with a what-a-shame shake.

"Even Britney never had it this bad. And, trust me, Britney—you know, she had it *real* bad."

Abby snapped the window curtains shut and faced Peter, who sat slumped on the couch. Two uneaten plates of scrambled egg whites and full glasses of orange juice sat on the coffee table. "I know it's hard, sweetie," she said. "But, really. You're better off without her."

Peter stared blankly at the TV as an old rerun of a teen sitcom played with the volume turned down. To Peter, the actors looked almost annoyingly happy. Fresh. Young. Innocent. Any problems they might possibly have (such as in this episode where so-and-so got caught kissing so-and-so and was, like, soooo embarrassed!) could be solved within the thirty-minute sitcom format. Tied up in a neat bow and free to return to their superficial bliss. One of the actors sported a gel-sculpted hairdo and an adorable smile, revealing a set of perfectly straight, white teeth. The tall, handsome teen actor was, in fact, Peter.

The irony of the moment wasn't lost on Peter, yet it wasn't even registering on Abby. "You saw the evidence," she continued, not even looking at the TV. "Consider yourself lucky. That girl could have really screwed with you if this deception went on any longer. It is what it is, and we will just move on."

> *It is what it is*
> *It ain't what it was*
> *Just a little boy lost*
> *Paying a big boy cost*

Lyrics sprayed into Peter's brain with a fire-hose burst. These creative rushes had been happening a lot lately. Ever since he got to know Josie. And now he couldn't turn them off even if he tried. He didn't even have to write them down or record them as voice notes into his phone. They were lyrics that kept him up at night and awakened him feeling inspired—the kind of lyrics he wrote with "that girl."

"I'm sorry, Peter," Abby said. "I hate to see you go through this. But someone had to tell you. We're just protecting you. You have everything to lose. You're the star, and she's just a nobody high school kid."

Peter grabbed the remote from the nightstand and obnoxiously turned up the volume to over thirty, trying to drown out Abby's speech justifying why kicking "that girl" to the curb was for "the best."

To be fair, Abby wasn't saying anything that everyone in

the Twitterverse wasn't already shouting at @PeterMaxxNow in a lynch mob chorus.

DUMP THAT PSYCHO SLUT! . . . YOU'RE TOO GOOD FOR HER! . . . JOSIE? MORE LIKE "HO-SIE" . . . WE LOVE YOU, BUT WE HATE THIS HOMEWRECKER!!!

One particularly spiteful @PeterMaxxNow follower had even adopted the username "@JosieBrantSucks" and had amassed 72,345 followers. In just two hours.

It was easy for Peter to ignore his phone and not check Twitter. In this moment, however, it was impossible for him to escape Abby's inability to just . . . stop . . . talking. If his Southern gentleman father hadn't hammered it into his brain that he had to be polite, especially to women, Peter would have blown her off when she began ranting five minutes ago. But that wouldn't be the Maxx way. The Maxxes, his dad was always quick to remind him, boasted a high tolerance for emotional pain, and making music was a bandage, drugs, and surgery all wrapped in one.

"Like everything else we've been through together, we'll get through this," Abby went on, settling beside him on the couch, adjusting her shin-length skirt as she crossed her stubble-covered legs that Peter did his best to ignore. She pulled a stick of nicotine gum from her purse and dropped it into her mouth.

Silence.

Agitated, Abby pressed, "So, Peter. Did she sign the agreement or not?"

More silence.

She grabbed the remote out of his hands and turned off the flat-screen TV.

"The envelope we gave you, Peter," she pressed. "Did you give it to her? It's very important that you *gave it to her*." Abby paused. "And that she signed it."

Her question floated uncomfortably between them. Abby let out a breathy exhale of exasperation. "Oh, dear Lord," she muttered under her breath. "What a mess."

"Um, what time is it?" Peter asked.

Abby glanced at her phone. "Ten after four."

Peter's eyes stayed glued on the blank screen. "No," he said flatly. "I don't think so."

His publicist checked the time again. "It is. Look." She showed him the clock on her phone. "I just checked and . . ."

"No," Peter interrupted. "Actually, I think it's *time* for you to leave."

Abby's bottom jaw dropped as fast as the Tower of Terror ride at Disneyland. "Well, then," she huffed, standing up. "I need a freakin' cigarette."

Abby sprung to her feet, readjusted her skirt, and walked over to the table to grab her phone and purse.

"Okay, well, then," she said, clearly defeated. "See you at the airport."

"Wait, Abby. . . . I don't wanna be rude. I'm sorry. You know that I'm sorry, I just—" Peter didn't want to say too much. "I just have a lot of things I need to figure out, and having a bunch of adults telling me what I should or shouldn't be doing isn't helping."

"It's okay," she interrupted, touching his shoulder. "You've been under a lot of pressure. I get it." She checked her phone and said under her breath, "I obviously picked a bad week to quit smoking."

She walked back over to Peter, who still sat slumped on the couch, and rubbed his head.

When the door shut behind her, Peter lay down flat on his back on the bed. He kicked off his high-tops and took a deep breath. For the next several minutes, all that could be heard was the drone of the air conditioner. And his steady breath. A deep inhale of air through his nose, then out his mouth. With the release of air came the noise rattling from deep within his throat. Release. If singing was his therapy, deep breathing exercising was his therapist. No publicist. No bodyguard. No dad. No media. No fangirls. Nobody. Peace. Breathing.

Peter's phone then suddenly hopped to life with vibration on the coffee table. The happy-go-lucky text tone used to be music to his ears, the signal often being that a shy girl with dark eyes and bright spirit had sent him a message that would make him smile.

Peter pushed himself up off the couch and hustled over to read the message.

hey petey. Buck up.

Dad.

and do me a favor . . . stay off that Twitter machine.

Not exactly the text buddy he was hoping for.

40

"Grounded for life."

These three words from Josie's mom when Josie ambled into the apartment didn't surprise Josie. After all, she had A, lied to her mom about camping with her friends, B, driven off to Vegas with the bad-girl neighbor with whom she had been forbidden from being friends, and C, while in Sin City, managed to tarnish the family name even more than it was already. And, oh, D, acted like a total brat ever since her dad's arrest the week before.

But her mom, who only found out her daughter was in Vegas after getting dozens of Facebook messages from her friends alerting her, didn't strangle her the second she saw her. This *did* surprise Josie.

Considering she was basically behaving like the devil's spawn, Josie expected her mom to scream and shout and take away every privilege she enjoyed—besides eating and sleeping. But, much to Josie's pleasure, she didn't totally freak out. At least, at first.

But when Josie walked into her bedroom the first thing she noticed was that her computer was gone. Just then, her mother followed her inside and shut the door behind her.

Josie dropped into her bed, landing face-first into a puffy

white pillow.

"I am not perfect," her mom continued. "Far from it. And I don't expect you to be, either. But what I do expect from you is to show some respect for me. Some basic respect. But put aside the fact that you lied to me. Do you realize how dangerous it was for you to do what you did? You could have been lying dead on the side of a desert road somewhere and I would have no idea. The fact that you showed such poor judgment is just . . . is just . . ." Josie had never heard her mom so upset. "Just so not you! That is not the girl I raised. That is not the Josie Brant I know. And that drug-addict neighbor of ours, she is definitely gonna have hell to pay."

"She's not a drug addict!" Josie shouted. "She doesn't even do drugs."

"That's not what I'm told," her mother fired back. "That's not what the rest of the world has to say."

"Maybe I don't care what the rest of the world thinks." Josie got up from her bed and squared off with her mom. "Maybe I don't care what anyone thinks for a change. At least D listens to me. She respects me."

"If that girl had a respectful bone in her body she never would have driven you to Vegas," her mom said. "And while we're on the topic of respect, Peter Maxx clearly has none for you either. It's so sad that you were too blinded by hormones to see that one coming too."

Josie felt the urge to throw every available piece of anything within her reach in her room at the nearest wall.

She opted instead to hurl more words at her now panting mother.

"If *you* had a respectful bone in *your* body you wouldn't dismiss everything I have to say and blame my feelings on 'hormones.' Maybe that's why I just needed to get away. Maybe I just wanted someone to take me seriously."

⏮ ⏹ ⏭

The next morning, Josie sat catatonic on the couch watching MTV reruns with Connor, lyrics dancing inside her head.

> *Who were you? Who was I?*
> *Trusted you, now not nobody*
> *Certainly not a guy*

"You probably shouldn't go on the Web for a while," Connor said. "It's pretty brutal."

"Thanks, Conz, I appreciate it. And, hey, I'm sorry I've been such a raging bitch lately."

"That's okay," said Connor, adding with a giggle, "Mom still thinks it's hormones. She told me that again last night."

Josie grunted.

It was not even 9:00 a.m. but Josie had already showered, fully unpacked her suitcase, and taken down every Peter Maxx poster on her wall and thrown it in the Dumpster out back. Anyone who would automatically eject someone from their life without even listening to what they had to say didn't deserve her attention.

She remembered once seeing the investigative special

"Celebrity Obsession" on the Hot Hollywood channel, which reported a recent nationwide study found that one in three people fit the definition of a "celebrity worshiper" and that with access to celebs like nonstop paparazzi and Twitter, people can be deluded into thinking they are closer to celebs than they really are.

"Josie, Dad's on the phone!" Connor yelled from the hallway outside her bedroom.

Josie rushed to the phone and grabbed it from her mom, who flashed three fingers and whispered, "Three minutes."

"Hey, Dad," Josie said, out of breath, walking back to her bedroom for some privacy.

"Hi, baby."

"I take it Mom told you."

"She did."

"I messed up, Daddy." Josie began crying. "I messed up real bad."

"It's okay, princess," he said soothingly. "At least you're not in jail like me. Things could be worse."

Josie pushed a giggle out through her tears.

"How's it going in there?" she asked.

"Honestly, it's horrible, Josie. I want to get out of here as soon as possible. I'm not a criminal. I don't belong in this place. It's so hot and crowded in here. But your mom has been a saint, coming to visit me twice a week. Being locked away makes you appreciate everyone, everything, on the outside a helluva lot more."

"I wish I could come visit, but Mom says I gotta be eighteen."

"Trust me, you're not missing much. Being allowed inside jail is one privilege you should be happy about not having. I will see you soon enough."

"When?"

"My lawyer is trying to get bail reduced so we can afford to post it. Hopefully soon."

"I hope so, because I miss you, Dad."

"I miss you, too." His voice cracked with emotion. "Sounds like that boy broke your heart. It happens. Guys can be hard to figure out, trust me on that one. I'm far from an expert on relationships, as you know, but did I ever tell you about the first time I had my heart broken?"

"No, you forgot to share that one."

"Well, her name was Bailey, and she was the cutest little thing who lived down the street from me. She had long blond hair and big old blue eyes. I was so taken by her. She apparently didn't have good judgment because she let me take her to our freshman dance and even kissed me. I told her I loved her and she said she loved me."

"Dad, that sounds like a *sweet* story, silly."

"Oh, well, just let me finish. So, anyway, two days later she leaves me a letter in my mailbox—this was before e-mail—and it said, 'I don't like you anymore. I am breaking up with you. Sorry. See ya, Bailey.' My mom saw me standing in our front yard crying my eyes out and later that night when she was putting me to bed, I told her I would never, ever fall in love with any girl ever again. My mom just rubbed my forehead and told me something I will never forget. She said, 'Kyle, sometimes for your heart to be open to love, it has to be broken by love. It is a gift in disguise.'"

Josie choked back tears. It was quite simply the most adorable thing her father had ever told her.

"I just wish I was there to hug you and hold you," he continued. "Every daughter needs her dad, even if he is a screw-up, like me."

"I'll be okay, don't worry," she assured him.

"I've had a lot of time to think about things in here. And one thing I realized is that I have been trying really hard for the last few years to find happiness, a new passion to replace hockey, a new woman to replace your mother—something, really, to numb the pain of ending my career. Looking back, it was kinda hard to be thirty-five and washed up. So that's what the drinking was about and, well, that's what growing the pot out on the farm was all about, too. I just thought I could make a quick buck—for all of us, not just myself—and it was easy to do."

"You don't have to explain, Dad. I get it."

"You're right. I should shut up. Hey, you're gonna laugh, but I've actually been reading a lot in here too."

"You're right." She giggled. "I am so laughing!"

"Well, it's true."

Josie could hear a guard yell, "Time's up!"

"Listen, Josie. I gotta go. But I wanted to tell you that one of the books I got from the reading cart was a basic guide to Buddhism. And, well, I read something in it that I want to tell you, because it made me think of you. It says that the first truth of Buddhism is: 'Life is suffering.' I take that to mean that life's not perfect, and people aren't perfect. In fact, life hurts and you will feel suffering because of that. So what I wanted to tell you is that, um, there's no way you can go preventing life from bringing you pain, but what we can do, what you can do, is travel the path of dealing with the suffering better. Suffering is just part of the journey. So I know that you're feeling a lot of pain right now, but I want you to know that if you believe that it will get better, and that you just learn from your mistakes and move forward by making positive changes you will feel happier and, then, the next thing you know—"

The phone went dead.

> *You can run*
> *You can try to run from all the pain*
> *But the truth is that hurt is the push you need*
> *To make a change that keeps you from*
>   *going insane*

Josie got up from her bed, walked out to the kitchen to her mom's Dell computer, and turned it on.

She deleted her Twitter and Facebook accounts.

Delete. Delete. Delete. Delete. Delete. Delete.

She pressed the delete key over and over and over, a ritualistic cleansing of all the cyber-toxicity.

Off the grid: where Josie believed she could go to limit her suffering.

Before completely shutting down the computer, Josie went to delete her Gmail messages. When she scrolled to one enti-tled "Christopher Playlist," she clicked it open and inside sat several links that Christopher had sent her two days after the arrest out on the farm. She had forgotten to listen to the songs. But now she did.

"Just the Way You Are"—Bruno Mars
"Last Beautiful Girl"—Matchbox 20
"Secrets"—OneRepublic
"Lonely No More" (Acoustic)—Rob Thomas
"The Big Bang"—Rock Mafia

Christopher had played "The Big Bang" for her before, but now, after listening to it after all the other tunes he had sent her, she realized during the bridge of the song that Christopher was trying to send her a message. . . .

> *Take it from me, I don't wanna be*
> *Mummified*
> *Sometimes I feel so isolated*
> *I wanna die. . . .*
> *So baby, bring your body here*
> *Next to mine, next to mine. . . .*

She had heard "The Big Bang" a lot before on the radio and seen the video for it, the dreamy one where Miley Cyrus appears angelic in it. But as Josie listened to the thumping bass and drums and the passionate voice, the lyrics took on an all-new meaning.

> *Some people like to talk*
> *But I'm into doing*
> *What I feel like doing*
> *When I'm inspired*
> *So, if we take a walk down*
> *The beach tonight*
> *I bet we could light up the sky . . .*

Christopher had gone out on a limb and, since she hadn't even taken the time to listen to the songs, Josie felt like she had done the equivalent of snapping that limb in half and letting him fall to the ground like an overweight coconut.

The song wasn't quite yet over, and with the cell he had loaned her, Josie texted Christopher.

> hey amigo! Sorry I've been so MIA. Been crazy.
> But I miss u like crazy. We gotta talk. Need an
> old-fashioned amigo chat sesh asap!

When he didn't text back right away, Josie texted again.

> I finally heard your playlist! OMG. So sweet. SO
> SWEET. Let's talk, C-Lo!

When Christopher still didn't text, she walked back to the living room and flicked on the TV. But who was she kidding? She couldn't focus on anything. She needed to talk to Christopher. Maybe she was wrong. Maybe Ashley was right about them being destined to be more than just friends. Maybe it took making the mistake of chasing Peter to make her realize that the boy she really should be with was with her the entire time. But she didn't know if this was the case or not. It was a thought, a possibility—something she had never considered until now.

So she called him.

It went straight to voice mail.

"Hey, Christopher. It's me. Josie. Uh, I'm calling you in case you're not getting my texts for some reason. Okay, so, I just wanted to talk to you. All right. So, yeah. Just wish you would text or call me back or something." Josie paused and exhaled into the phone. "Anyway, well, I miss you. Call me. Bye."

Josie had always thought of herself as anything but lonely. She had her music. She had her gadgets. Her bedroom, after all, was a kinetic hub of multimedia connectivity and telecommunications that forty years ago probably had enough microprocessing power to launch a rocket to the moon.

But now she lay back on her mattress, the same one she had since she was eleven, her feet dangling off the edge like she was a giant, feeling completely, utterly, desperately alone. And, more than she ever would have expected, she missed Christopher.

Going off the grid might not be as easy as she thought. When she graduated middle school the previous spring, her dad bought her a new iPhone, her mom gifted her an iPod Touch (the one that holds 32 gigs, enough to fit her 2,345 songs), and her grandma in Toronto (God bless her soul) sent her a MacBook. Ever since, her laptop had been her portal to the rest of the world, the machine that, even more than her phone, she would die without.

And on her laptop screensaver had flashed a series of pictures of her and Christopher, hugging each other in front of the Golden Gate Bridge while on a drama club trip to San Francisco the fall of her freshman year. The Two Amigos.

Christopher was the furthest thing from a cool "bro," and he didn't even hang out much with the drama nerds or band geeks, though he did play trumpet and designed sets for the fall and spring productions. Christopher knew more about music than anyone she knew within the Bakersfield city limits. But most impressive to Josie: Christopher possessed the equivalent of a PhD in '90s rockology. Sublime, Nirvana, Pearl Jam, Matchbox 20, Smashing Pumpkins, Chris Isaak, Radiohead, The Verve, Weezer, Goo Goo Dolls, Blink-182, Sheryl Crow, Dave Matthews Band.

Christopher had sat her down one afternoon and played her his entire '90s playlist. The country music her dad always played had decent enough lyrics, but the music part had that hillbilly sound to it. The '90s music Christopher played, however, lyrically told relatable stories *and* sounded cool.

One day after school, Christopher sat her down at the coffee shop and flipped open his laptop. "As a female, you need to know about Sheryl," he said.

"Sheryl?" Josie asked her tutor.

"Crow," he said matter-of-factly. "Sheryl Crow—hands

down, the best female singer-songwriter of the '90s."

He opened up a folder on his desktop titled "Goddesses."

"Just ask your mom," he continued.

"My mom doesn't like music."

"Everyone likes music," he replied. "Just not everyone *appreciates* music."

Christopher then gently placed his white earbuds into Josie's tiny ears and proceeded to play her every track from Sheryl Crow's 1993 debut album *Tuesday Night Music Club*. The songs blew Josie away.

But now, her personal rockologist/philosopher was gone. Like Ashley. Like Peter. Like her dad.

The last few years she already had been suffering from a profound sense of abandonment. And, in some twisted act of counterproductiveness, she had reacted by abandoning everyone who loved her . . . only to then be abandoned by everyone for real. The cycle had come full circle. Karma was biting her on the butt. And it stung like a bitch.

Christopher, the one person who she could always rely on to text or call immediately, was clearly not getting back to her. And though it pained her deeply, she couldn't blame him.

Just then, her doorbell rang and Josie shot up and ran to the front door and squinted through the peephole. The person was standing too close to the door to see their face, but she could make out what looked like yellow flower petals. Her heart racing, Josie whipped open the door, and greeting her on the doorstep was a pair of the kindest, most gentle eyes peering over a blossom of sunflowers. Instinctively, Josie extended her arms straight out and enveloped him.

"BBFF," she gasped, holding on to Christopher so tightly he looked as if he could suffocate. She then stepped back and took the flowers from him. "Awww, they're perfect. Totally perfect."

Josie closed the door and joined him on the porch. "I'd invite you in, but I'm not allowed to have anyone over," she said quietly. "Grounded for life."

"Ah, GFL. Harsh. I figured. That's why I came over. You probably won't be hitting up Starbucks anytime soon."

Josie grabbed hold of his arm.

"Christopher, I'm sorry. I've been a total idiot. I became that stupid girl who changed herself for a guy—something I always swore I would never do. I was being ridiculous."

Christopher couldn't hold back a laugh.

"What's so funny?" Josie asked.

"I saw the paparazzi pics from yesterday. That outfit was pretty ridiculous."

"I can't disagree. I don't know what I was thinking."

"You were thinking you were in love. You're a romantic. You're a hopeless romantic, Josie Brant. That's why you're such a great songwriter. You have a heart the size of California."

"If I had a heart, I would have been more sensitive to yours. I promise I will be better. I will be a better friend."

Christopher stuck his hands in the front pockets of his jeans and fixed his gaze at her.

"I finally listened to your playlist," Josie said.

Christopher shrugged his shoulders. "Forget about it. It was just a moment. It passed."

"It was so sweet. Those songs. I mean, your friendship means the world—"

"Amigo." He interrupted her and took a breath. "Please stop with the F word already!"

"What?"

"Friend this, friend that. I get it. We are *friends*."

"I don't mean it like that," she insisted. "Really."

"Well, I don't wanna be your lover. I'll leave that to the pop stars."

"Yeah, right. That's just working out great for me."

"Seriously," Christopher added. "Don't worry. I've decided that our friendship is more important to me. I don't want to lose that. You know, now all we should wanna do is have a little fun."

"Sheryl?"

"Duh, obviously." He laughed.

Josie didn't believe Christopher. His eyes told a different story.

"The reason I came over was to tell you that, yeah, I *was* hurt. But not any longer. I'm still here for you. I just wanted to make sure you were doing okay. Friends forever?"

"But maybe someday we could be something more than friends," Josie blurted out. "Maybe I'm just confused."

"No." Christopher shook his head. "We're not meant to be

that way. I'm happier this way. We are both happier."

"But if it makes us so happy—" Josie sang in her best Sheryl Crow voice.

"Then why the hell are we so sad?"

"Exactly," she said.

"Because letting go of something that makes you feel bad usually hurts the most."

Josie hugged him again. This time, he reciprocated. His tight embrace seemed to squeeze tears from her eyes.

"And, oh," he added, releasing her. "Happy birthday tomorrow."

41

The buzzing phone on the mattress bolted Josie awake. Still half asleep, she answered it.

"Hello?" she groaned.

"Josie?" a male voice said.

"Yeah." She sat up in bed. "Yes, this is Josie."

"I just wanted to call and wish you a Happy Birthday."

"Peter?"

"Yes."

Josie's eyes popped open wide. All she could muster was a groggy, "Okaaaay."

"I guess I can't call you 'Almost 15' anymore," Peter said.

"No, you can't."

#Awkward.

"I'm not only calling to wish you a Happy Birthday, Josie. I'm also calling to say I'm sorry. Truly. I jumped to conclusions, made assumptions—before I had all the facts straight. And now I do have all the facts straight. And I apologize."

"But, Peter, I told you the facts: I didn't do it!" Being able to face her accuser, Josie felt empowered for the first time since the whole ordeal went down. And she vented. "You've always had the facts. You just chose to believe all your so-called 'people'—and not me."

"You're right, Josie. Everything I said about wanting to be my own person, doing what I want to do and thinking for myself—it all went out the window. I messed up."

Josie let his words soak into the silence between them.

"You did. And even though I want to tell you it is okay, that I am over it, that I understand, the truth is that I don't. I'm not even sure I want to talk to you right now."

"Wait, Josie, don't hang up!"

Josie gritted her teeth and got up out of her bed.

"I don't expect you to forgive me, Josie, but I wanted to tell you that what I did was wrong. Very wrong. And you deserve a lot better. Anyone deserves better, but especially you. What I said on the stage in Vegas is true, Josie. You're my muse. I want you back in my life." He exhaled into the phone; Josie could almost feel his warm breath. "And I'm not taking no for an answer."

"That's a really beautiful thing to say, but why should I believe you? Why should I trust anything you say?"

"Well, for the same reason that I should have always trusted you. Because I think we are just meant to be together. I want to write great love songs with you. I want our life to be a love song."

"Wow, you really know how to charm a girl," she said, her voice turning more serious. "The problem is that the rest of the world hates my guts. All thanks to you."

Josie was just getting warmed up. She hopped off her mattress and began pacing her room.

"I can't believe that you, suddenly, call me out of the blue and assume that you can throw me under the bus, kick me out of your life like some cheap groupie, and then ask me to get over it just because you call me up and tell me I am your muse? It doesn't work that way. I don't care if you're the most famous teenager in the world."

"That's not what I expected at all," Peter said. "What I expected was a strong girl, with a strong sense of herself, to stand up for herself and tell me to go to hell. That is the Josie I expected."

"Well, then your dream has come true! The problem is that, realistically, no matter what you think, the rest of the world thinks I'm a shady homewrecker."

"Not for long they won't."

"What do you mean?"

"Let's just say I have a special birthday present for you. Are you near a computer?"

"No. My mom hid my laptop because she doesn't think it's a good idea for me to go on the Web right now. And, I have to say, I agree with her."

"You guys are wrong," Peter said sharply.

"Yeah, right. Easy for you to say."

"I'm not kidding. Your phone has Web, right?"

"Yeah."

"Just, please, do me a favor. Hang up and go to Hot Hollywood's website."

"And what will I see there?"

"Just trust me."

EXCLUSIVE! Peter Maxx's Ex-GF Exposed as a Secret Tabloid Source, Federal Probe Underway

Today 6:40 A.M. PDT by Jackson Phillips,
Hot Hollywood Chief News Correspondent

After being exposed by an investigation led by Peter Maxx's longtime bodyguard, G Girls singer and ex-girlfriend of Maxx, Sandy Jones, was immediately fired from the group and now faces federal criminal charges for allegedly hacking into Maxx's cell phone and accessing his e-mail account so that she could leak information to the gossip website OMC.

In an exclusive interview with Hot Hollywood to air in its entirety tonight, Maxx reveals that he had broken up with Sandy Jones before even meeting the Bakersfield, California, high school student, Josie Brant. "My security team, led by Big Jim, uncovered that Sandy sent OMC false and misleading information with the goal of making her look like a victim and making me look like a jerk."

When reached by Hot Hollywood via phone and asked if he was aware that many of his so-called "scoops" were the result of potentially illegal activity and he could himself face charges (and deportment as he is a British citizen), OMC's normally outspoken Editor-in-Chief Johnny Love replied with a terse "no comment."

In his sit-down with Hot Hollywood, Maxx further explained, "Sandy and I had made the mistake of not being honest with our fans and revealing that we were no longer dating. I regret that decision, but promise not only to make it up to my fans with a series of upcoming free concerts, but also make it up to Josie Brant, who is an amazing girl and unfortunate victim of a false attack on her character. You will be hearing and seeing a lot more from Josie Brant."

When asked whether he and Josie Brant were still romantically attached, Maxx relayed, "That's something I am trying to figure out. But I hope so. If I have my way, you will be seeing more of Josie Brant, who is a very talented songwriter. She is, quite simply, my muse."

Three months later . . .

Josie and Peter both learned a hard lesson of the Internet Age: the hammer of public opinion can strike with powerful force—for good and for bad.

As much as Josie had been demonized by the media, now they adored her.

Fans, meanwhile, launched blogs, Tumblrs, Twitter accounts, and Pinterest and Facebook pages dedicated to the pony-tailed teenager with the sweet brown eyes. So many girls simply related to her, felt she was just a regular girl who had been betrayed by a psycho-chick. Many even started dressing like her. Jeans, TOMS sneakers, baseball caps, message T-shirts, and all. Blondes even started to dye their hair brown . . . hoping they too could snag the affections of Peter Maxx. But, of course, the pop star had eyes for only one brunette.

And thanks to Peter's tell-all interview with Hot Hollywood (and some crack investigative work by Big Jim), the public was starting to find out what Peter had known all along: that Josie was a gifted songwriter. In fact, Peter proudly announced that he and Josie were cowriting a new album together that would be out just in time for Christmas.

But, now, Josie was about to reveal another talent.

Josie sat in a dressing room at L.A.'s Staples Center, a makeup artist putting on the final touches of bronzer and eye shadow as a hairstylist sprayed her hair into perfect place. She wore a black T-shirt with the word "love" embroidered on the chest in shiny beads and red-and-white kicks that stuck out from underneath the bottom pant legs of her skinny jeans.

In the mirror, she could see sitting behind her on the couch Connor, her mom, and Delilah, who, thanks to casting that Harry Potter spell on her during that Vegas trip, was majorly responsible for the fearlessness she was about to show by doing what she was about to do. Ever the loyal BBFF, Christopher also wandered around the room, documenting every moment with the camera on his phone.

Next to the couch stood a handsome man in blue jeans and a perfectly ironed dress shirt. Josie locked eyes with him in the mirror as the makeup artist dabbed her with more bronzer. The man snapped a picture of her with his phone.

"Please, Dad," Josie said. "Don't you think we've had enough with the paparazzi?"

A day earlier, Peter had posted the $5 million bail, setting Kyle Brant free.

For the first time in seemingly forever, everyone Josie loved most was in one place with her. Everyone, that is, but for one person—though his voice was vibrating through the walls of the arena, rattling Josie's chest just as it had the very first time she heard him sing.

Then, Peter's dad stepped into the dressing room and announced, "Showtime!"

Bobby handed her a wireless microphone. Josie then went around the room and hugged everyone. She couldn't look her mom and dad in the eyes, though. She didn't want their tears to make her cry and ruin her perfectly applied makeup. Josie took one last glance in the dressing room mirror and, for the first time in a very long time, liked every inch she saw.

Josie followed Bobby down the hallway and climbed a set of stairs to the edge of the stage, where she stood behind a curtain. She could hear Peter gently strumming his guitar.

"Well, honey, you sure do look like a pop star," Bobby told her.

"Maybe," Josie said with a smile. "But I'm still just a fan."

Acknowledgments

My heartfelt thanks to the team it took to write and
    research this story day and night
Are most fittingly delivered in the form of lyrics,
    all right?

Michael, Miriam, and Jane—my literary agency crew
Who knew, who could see
Even when I didn't yet hear the music in me

Loving encouragement from friends and family—
    Jackson, Chloe, and Brooke, as I took
Time and space to explore the characters in this book

Tim James and Antonina Armato, Rock Mafia
    (all of you, to be sure)
Miley, Selena, Jonas, Justin, pop stars at the creative core
Lisa Cheng and Running Press pushing for more

God, Goaltending, the Paynes, Matt Riley, observed
    Beach Cities teens, y'all in Bakersfield
Twitterverse, Aurora, Kris, and Chris
A BFF whose friendship knows no yield

Every love song ever written
Every crush to have ever bitten
Everyone at E!
Everyone who cares about me

Anonymous lovers in the category of "was"
Inspiration amid this hopeless romantic's endless
    Coffee Bean buzz

About the Author

Ken Baker is E! Entertainment Television's chief news correspondent. Ken has interviewed or reported on just about every major pop star in the world—all of whom he proudly has on his playlist. Follow him @kenbakernow.